not everyone wants roses

Not Everyone
Wants Roses
Jen Poteet

DEDICATION

To everyone who loves true crime

We bathe in our own blood
at the moon's whimsy

And they wonder why
we aren't afraid of it

CONTENTS

CHAPTER 1

Siri, play Sad Girl Morning Mix

It's a nondescript Wednesday. Smack dab in the middle of my routine week where the days are broken into single shift days, double duty days and the sacred day off Sunday. Donned in my navy-blue vest, I have yet again convinced my thick thighs to carry me into the cold as a crypt building instead of running into the nearby patch of trees to sweet freedom. Let's be honest, I am not exactly the live off the land type.

Every day, millions of people just like me clock in to work at big corporate retailers. Lured by fancy words like health insurance and retirement benefits, the kind of benefits that are not always a guarantee with jobs these days. Especially for kindred spirits who have never wanted to go to college because we could not think of what we wanted further education on. Particularly if also like me, imagining sitting in one place for hours and hours will cause hive breakouts and anxiety induced perspiration. If these people are lucky (again like myself), they work in a super-duper deluxe version of corporate retailer and get the bonus of being able to get a set of acrylic nails, their hair did, body hair removed by hot wax, taxes filed and even see an optometrist.

Yawning, I shuffle into the nail salon. Quinn and Tillie not only manage this specific establishment they have an ingenious side hustle.

"Good morning, Faye," the identical twins sing song from behind an espresso machine tucked in the back corner. Though my body usually cringes away from too much dairy, it has no problem enjoying their combination of espresso with sweetened condensed milk. Though they have lived in the States for over a decade, the special drink is a recipe from their origin country of Vietnam. Looking me over, Quinn adds, "You look like shit, you wanna extra shot?"

"Good morning to you, too. No thanks, an ER visit has a thousand-dollar copay," I reply, and throw a few extra dollars in their collection jar.

"I see you tomorrow for a fill, right?" Tillie asks.

"Yes ma'am." I wave over my shoulder as I head to the back room to punch the time clock and count my till.

There are more staff than usual milling about and confusion must be written all over my face.

"Mandatory meeting this morning, Queen." Dontae blinks at me. "It was in the weekly email."

I respond intelligently with, "People read those?" Then I follow my work bestie to a far wall to lean against. There are some chairs. I prefer to be away from everyone but a select few. Dontae takes advantage of our proximity and begins rummaging through the pocket of my vest, his long nails clack together. I snatch myself away. "Git!"

"Come on, I know you've got pocket snacks," he whines.

"Peanut butter crackers...not a complimentary continental breakfast," I mumble.

"Ahem." Our store manager clears his throat to get everyone's attention. Everything about this man is short and stubby. From his hands sprout ten Vienna sausages. I have had the misfortune of seeing his toes at a team building event where the offensive piggies were on full display in flip flops. *Flip flops.* Fluorescent light washes him out like most of us sitting here, in this room that always smells like an old gym sock with hints of onion.

On my left I feel the hot laser beam of an unwavering gaze. This man has long, sturdy appendages and I need no imagination to picture all of them because I in times of weakness have taken him home. For all intents and purposes, he is a fine catch. Fairly easy on the eyes with his stock room muscles. Testosterone wafts off him in waves. I blame biology for recognizing his virile masculinity and being interested solely because he has the ability to hunt my food and build me a shelter. But he is so damn boring. A fine, boring man.

"Put him out of his misery," Dontae whispers to me. Somehow the offensive lighting does not wash out his rich skin. His glossed lips twinkle as he laughs at me.

I elbow him. "Enough of that," I drawl, but it only makes him laugh harder.

As Manager McStubbs drones on and on about corporate shit that none of us cares about, I completely space out. I imagine I'm on a beach. No, I'm in a jungle. A jungle beach, with a drink in my hand that is made up of an entire coconut. Little umbrellas and more fruit decorate the fuzzy sides. In real life it would be impossible to lift and it would taste like sunscreen, but in my head, it is light as a feather and doesn't. The shushing lullaby of waves increase my dopamine and are scientifically proven to lower cholesterol. My pale complexion is shaded by a comically large palm frond held by a cabana man. Gray sprouts from his temples because now that I am over thirty, I am into that sort of thing. He speaks only two phrases in English, "Can I get you another drink?" and "Would you like foot massage?" I am about to fantasize about a good foot rub, when the sounds of clapping ruin my daydream.

"Come back to Earth Ass-tronaut," Dontae says sarcastically and I realize everyone is looking directly at me.

"Come on up, Faye," Stubby says. Reluctantly, I drag myself to his side and take the contents from his damp hands. "Happy fifteen-year anniversary!" he says, and the clapping ensues.

Oh.

My face heats at the attention but I manage to offer a smile and accept the store gift card to the place I have spent a decade and half working at—and the gold pin that declares this achievement.

"All right guys, let's move in for a hand stack!" our manager exclaims happily, like this ritual is not mildly humiliating. I hate the hand stack, but of course, I do the damn hand stack.

I attached my newly acquired flare next to my name tag. Corporate makes us wear them, even though we are usually addressed as "Hey you!" or my personal favorite, "Do you work here?" No, once upon a time I came to this place and was so enamored by the polyester blue smocks I just had to get one for myself. It brings out my veins.

Dontae and I have teased each other about going "next door" to the big box home improvement store. We figured the customers would be, if not hotter, at least manlier. In the end there are only so many "Wow that's a lot of wood you've got there!" and "You looking for a good screw?" jokes we could make, and the laughs wouldn't be worth all the mansplaining we would most likely get. As much as I love to bitch about this place it actually is not that bad. I make enough to not live with my parents, I have plenty of extra to buy true crime books and streaming services and kibble for my cat R.B. (Though he prefers to eat small animals.) Besides, here I get variety.

The chiming of the scanner marks time faster than a clock's ticking hands, and I get to play my favorite game. This game consists of me imagining what customers are doing with the contents of their shopping cart. Obviously, some are cut and dry. *Maybe feed your shoe full of kids something other than cereal and frozen chickee nuggs, lady.* Then, I have a little old crone come through my lane who is buying fuck tons of candles. Okay, are we hiding the scent of a rotting corpse with these, or summoning a demonic entity who loves the scent of vanilla? As I ring my next customer, I try to make pleasantries over his multiple containers of, like, natural personal lubricant. I say "Have a nice day!" when I hand him his change but what I mean is "Good luck with whatever you're planning." God speed. But then I get a lady counting pennies while tears stream down her face, trying to find enough to purchase the pink birthday cake on the conveyor belt. She is so sad it bursts my fun bubble, so I tell her it won't scan so she can just take it and then put my own money in the till when she is gone. It is the end of the month, and this is just one of many plights of the working class. If she stays poor enough, the receiver of that cake gets free health insurance and coupons for milk and fresh vegetables. But if she makes more than what the good ol' U.S. of A considers the poverty level, she will lose her benefits and probably be in my two-job shoes. Then she will never be home to see her family. I'm somber until lunch.

Like most adult friendships, I made unbreakable bonds at work. These friends and I may have never crossed paths in the real world but here in this industrial sized shit show we found each other and held on tight. Being thrust together with people I may not have met otherwise has also led me to other relationships. Specifically one, and he is staring at me again because of course he is taking his lunch break at the same time. I let out a sigh because I have put this conversation off for too long, "Hey, Wyatt."

He scratches his thick beard before replying, "Hey," in his timber, pine, lumberjack deep voice. He is even wearing a red flannel for goodness sakes.

"So, look," I begin, awkward as fuck, "we had some good times, right? But truthfully you need a nice girl. Not someone like me." It isn't a lie. I take great care of myself and can admit I am a little vain for it, but with my affinity for the color black and anything coffin shaped, I am not everyone's cup of tea. In fact, I am not even tea. I'm more like the stagnant coffee in the cup you have left sitting in the console of your car for two weeks.

Wyatt is nice. He deserves white picket fences to hold-in his future brood of equally giant sons, and while I know he would be content to try to plant them in me, motherhood just isn't in the cards. The same affliction that keeps me waxing body hair off my chest and face is the same one that will make getting pregnant hard. Which is all right with me, but that doesn't mean my heart is not going out to all the women with their legs over their heads and their fingers crossed. Wyatt just continues to stare at me contemplatively, like he is an adolescent girl, and I am a wild free-range pony. No one has been able to tame Midnight Sally, she's just too wild. Too addicted to the brush of wildflowers on her flanks as she runs breakneck speed through the fields. But Lord willing he'll try. Maybe he is picking up what I'm putting down but maybe not. He is certainly a strong reliable tool, but not the sharpest in the shed. The way he is looking at me, though, it is clear he is thinking about how I do not have many other dudes knocking at my door. Which is true, I don't. Whatever. I'm not hungry anymore.

My bad mood worsens as the day continues. The best part of working for "the man" is they give you a ton of breaks. I'm on my third and last of the day when Dontae sidles up beside me. "You look a little lost. Need some spiritual guidance?" he asks, while simultaneously pulling the stack of tarot cards from his own dress code required vest. I nod as he cuts the deck seven times before fanning the cards out in front of me. I have played this game enough to know his moves. I scan the lot before I feel the admittedly slightly off-putting pull towards one and pinch the corner between my fingers before I gently pull it out.

"Ah shit," I whisper to the skeleton dancing on the card's face.

"The Death card doesn't always mean a literal death," Dontae reassures me, "but change is coming whether you like it or not. You gotta let some shit go."

"You work tonight, Queen?" Dontae asks as I collect my things to high tail it out of here.

"It's Karaoke night..." I deliver in the same tone a doctor would say you have weeks to live, "...aka Y2K country countdown...aka high school reunion the musical."

His eyes sparkle with mischief. "Maybe I'll come and mix it up with my 'w.a.p.'" He makes the 'p' audibly pop and twerks his backside against my thigh.

"I look forward to seeing you later then," I say before making my way towards the exit and into the humid South Carolina air. My feet move on their own accord and just as I have done every day in the last eleven months, I stop in front of the missing person's board. "Have you seen me?" The question makes me nauseous. No, I have not, Mandy, and I miss you so much I physically ache. You stare out from the faded photocopied paper like a ghost. They used the picture I took of you on your twenty-ninth birthday. Your smile stretches across your face so full of joy and life it mocks me now because in my heart I know something terrible has happened to you.

XIII
Death

CHAPTER 2

I'll take Childhood Induced Trauma for 100

Mandy and I met during first day on the job orientation, both of us seventeen at the time. She wore all pink and was bubbly and I wore all black and was not. Despite having almost nothing we liked in common; she became my best friend.

The year we turned twenty-five we drove South to visit beach towns in Florida. After the trip we started saving to relocate, even though I am not into sun or sand. For whatever reason Mandy thought moving somewhere even more hot and more humid would solve all our problems. But once we moved out of the houses we grew up in and into our own apartments, most of our problems were gone. Turns out there is a thing called 'situational depression.'

My parents are not the well-off type, but as working middle class, they've done all right. My childhood home is a rambler with a little wear and tear. Most projects never get done because home improvements come with hefty costs, but my parents have maintained what they could. There is a magnolia growing on the front lawn, its sturdy branches always held me despite my mother's opinion on the matter.

The carpet has gone thin, but I still kick my shoes off at the door out of habit. My father sits in the hospital bed that has replaced his old recliner, the television remote in his gnarled hand.

"It's my favorite girl!" he calls out, even though my mother is not five steps away in the kitchen and I have a younger sister. *Thanks Dad, that does not make me uncomfortable at all.*

"Yep, I've got your favorite girl alright." I set down the bag of Little Debbie snack cakes on his bedside table among the pill bottles and kiss his sallow cheek. Watching him waste away slowly over the last several months has been hell. Hospice stops by daily, and so do I. Some days it is a check in—others I stay longer to relieve those who live here and watch him round the clock.

"You shouldn't feed him that junk," my mother says in lieu of a normal greeting. Just the sound of her voice makes me cringe. Everything about me drives her insane and the feeling is mutual. I was hoping she would be at work.

She constantly critiques my appearance. The woman has been a hairdresser her whole life and a former beauty pageant contender, so looks are very important to her. She is dainty and feminine, two adjectives no one would use to describe me, and it has been one of many sources of our bickering. I do not want to fight in front of Dad, so I just let her go on. In one ear and out the other. I drown out her actual words with internal screaming. The dying inhuman screeching of a thousand's-year-old vampire feeling the fatal kiss of sun rays before it bursts into a pile of glitter.

I could say my mother is passive aggressive and you may wonder how someone can be passive yet aggressive simultaneously. If you are just 'aggressive aggressive' like me people call you a bitch, but when you do it subtly, passively, it is somehow more palatable. For instance, I am wearing my favorite earrings. They are meat cleavers, whose plastic blades are filled with a red sparkly gelatinous substance. I purchased them from the seasonal Halloween store that set up shop in what was a roller rink last year. They are fabulous and bring me joy. My mother says things like, "You know, Faye, you shouldn't wear those because people will think there's something wrong with you."

Good, I am deranged. Stay far, far away.

Other unsolicited criticism of the day has included my hair, which is parted down the middle and in two space buns atop my head. She says the style is childish. She doesn't voice her dislike of the snake tattooed on my forearm, the pumpkins permanently inked on my thigh, or the other tattoos I have—anymore. Thankfully, my mother just curls her lip in disgust. But my clothes are always fair game. She starts on my outfit, a crop top and high waisted jeans that are stretchy and feel like a warm hug to my abdomen. "You know, Faye, if I was your size I wouldn't wear clothes that bring attention to...certain areas."

Ironically, I have better self esteem than she does, and these "certain areas" are fine by me.

"I only say these things because I don't want anyone to hurt you and if I'm thinking this, they probably are thinking it too. People can be so mean." She goes on and on and it's her, she's people. Because she is the only person who has ever said this kind of shit to me. My mother claims she does not want anyone to hurt my feelings, yet she is the one always saying ignorant shit.

The worst part of it all? The same rosebud lips she paints in Valentine's Day colors and spew her hateful words are the same exact ones I have on my own face. We share more than this feature, and the older I get the more her image looks back at me in the mirror and I fucking hate it so much. Maybe that is what turned me goth in the end, or just that she hates my style so much it makes me like it more. Just call me Petty Betty.

"What's on?" I ask my dad even though I know it is a game show.

"Wanna watch this?" he asks as he enjoys the layered waxy black and white cake. I do not know why you would deny someone on their deathbed anything. That is why I bring him junk food. He is already dying; a few extra preservatives are not going to make anything worse.

"Where's Scarlet?" I ask after my younger sister and sit on the hideous floral love seat next to his bed.

"She's at work," my mother calls from the kitchen even though I was not talking to her. Scarlet is the apple of my mother's eye. My sister followed her high heeled footsteps into the cosmetology industry. She still lives here in our childhood home with her boyfriend and their two young children. Speaking of which, it is awful quiet. "Where are the babies?" I ask after the two terrors who have littered the living room with their toys.

"Nap time," my sister's boyfriend answers as he flops down on the love seat cushion beside me. It used to irk the shit out of me that they had not found their own place and yet continued to procreate before my dad got sick. But I cannot find it in my cold black heart to hate her unemployed sperm donor. He cuts the grass. He does the heavy lifting. He gives my dad a shower. Kyle.

Like every Kyle, Kevin, and Brandon he is decent looking if your taste is 'generic white boy.' Complete with a cornucopia of terrible tattoos and a preference to white tank tops as upper body wear to show off aforementioned tasteless body art. I hate to stereotype but he is a walking one, with his deftly cut sideburns and six pack of energy drinks. He is a jack of all trades but master of nothing at all. Kyle, and guys just like him, have one true superpower and it is their fertility magic. They shake your hand all the while making direct eye contact and say, "Wow, you're so beautiful!" and damn if you aren't having one of their babies a few months later. Albeit you have perfectly functioning ovaries, unlike myself. My sister got this one right out of high school, so he did not have ample time to impregnate the county.

"How's it going, Sissy?" Kyle asks, eating one of the cakes I brought my dad. Washing it down with something that is ruining his liver but energizing him through his day of doing God only knows what. He calls me Sissy because Scarlet calls me Sissy, a nickname from days gone by. Back before our parents created this weird animosity between us for having favorites. Her our mom's and me our dad's. It is weird to think that any day now the person who loves me the most in the world will no longer be in the world. I will put that bag of feelings where I put all the other unwanted ones, deep down in the murder basement of my mind. It has dirt floors and everything.

"All good, my dude," I reply while the three of us sit companionably.

I stay as long as I can, shouting answers to the idiots playing on screen, and exist in this space with my dad because there is going to come a day real soon that I will not be able to.

CHAPTER 3

Today's Special:
Pulled Pork Platter $9.99

If you have never worked in food service, this may not be common knowledge to you. But in every bar, restaurant, bistro, café, or whatever establishments across America there is a day crew and a night crew. Day crew opens the doors, handles the old folks, the lunch breakers and the day drinkers. They are usually finishing their menial tasks like rolling silverware or marrying ketchups while the night crew settles in for the main event. Most weekdays the servers can handle the bar themselves but on the few busy nights of the week they get lil' ol' me.

There are many versions of how this place got its name, most of them surrounding what the original name was. Whether it was *The Watering Hole, Hole in the Wall,* or my personal favorite *The Glory Hole,* it is now just 'The Hole.' Despite the name, this building is an impenetrable fortress that has been standing for ages serving generation after generation libations. A glorified lean-to held together by hopes and dreams and surely built upon a ley line because of its magical aversion to time and weather. If you were to Google "dive bar" the image of this place would fill your screen and damn if it isn't applicable to another truth, these places have the best food, *The Hole* included.

There is a back door to enter directly into the kitchen, specifically the damp towel scented dishwashing nook. Keeping the flies out is just a screen door I do not even try not to slam, the spring sprung so tightly. Next to the double sinks our bus boy jumps, so I cackle. He is barely old enough to work as late and as long as his work permit permits. But he is old enough to be in a romantic relationship with a cephalopod, the only logical explanation for the circular suction marks all over his neck. He does not even pretend to squirt me with the dish sprayer anymore since I have locked him in the walk-in fridge a few times. Terror builds character.

Around the bend are the stoves, the flat top grill, and a few metal prep worktables.

"Miss Irene!" I greet as she sits in a chair, her body spilling over the sides. Her weight does not allow for much mobility, but every day she comes to work, makes it to that very spot, cuts, shreds, mixes, and picks whatever the kitchen needs.

"Miss Innes." I make my way to the cooktop where the small statured octogenarian stirs today's special. Innes is a magician. She has this way of making food you have eaten your whole life taste so good you wonder what the hell you have been eating all this time.

"Come get a bite before you get to work," she says, her voice as light and airy as her skeleton. Any given time she is either trying to feed me or teach me how to cook. Miss Innes swears one day I will meet someone who I will want to cook something from scratch for. Sarcastic asshole that I am, I tell her not to hold her breath.

"Just a small bowl, I'm holding out for the peach cobbler." I most definitely do not diet but I have to watch what I eat, or it will go to my hips, or my face will break out. Thanks to my genetic affliction.

"Maybe one day you'll cook for me." Her hands do not look like they would be so soft with all their wrinkles, but they are like silk as she places the bowl in my hand. Fifty-fifty coleslaw and her famous vinegar-heavy South Carolina pork barbecue.

"Nah, I'm selfish." I kiss her temple in thanks. "Innes, you gotta get new kicks." The big toe on her left foot is sticking out of her worn sneakers.

"I had to get a tire, so I'll go next check." As she replies I pull out the gift card I got today.

"Here you go, this should cover it." I slip it into the front of her apron before she can protest. "As thanks."

I am saved from further argument as Donna, one of our waitresses, comes halfway through the kitchen door, "Babydoll, you gotta get out here the bar is full already and I've got fucking tables." She is there and gone in a moment, leaving the door swinging back and forth on its hinges. Donna is the always wound-tight type. Donna is ageless: meaning her actual age is unknown. Her face is lined deeply from smoking as long as I have been alive, decades of fluorescent pink kissed cigarette butts litter the parking lot. She has given herself a tattoo with India Ink and a bobby-pin. To her everyone is Darling, Honey or Babydoll, but in truth she does not remember our names and hates us all. She is baddass and I love her despite her anxious aura.

I follow her out of the kitchen to the front of the house and scoot my way behind the L-shaped bar. Rocking Ricky, our resident Karaoke DJ, is setting up his equipment for tonight's weekly festivities of 'watching folks with way too much confidence make interesting life choices.' Katie, the other server scheduled tonight, comes behind the bar to pour a draft beer for her table while I finish getting myself together. "This one's about out. I'll grab Trevor," she says before leaving me to man my station. Katie and I graduated from the same high school, though we were never friends, we are friendly enough now.

Trevor, our bar back, has the physique of a stick bug but can carry a keg of beer which is literally his only job requirement. We get into heated arguments about music and film because his taste is shit. I call him names like Twat Waffle and Douche Bag as I yell at him, arms a-flailing. If anyone else talked to him in a similar fashion I would eat their faces off. I imagine my affection for him something akin to having a little brother. He changes the keg seamlessly while giving me the rundown of this semester's final grades as I slice lemons and limes.

The Hole's employees work together like cogs in a machine while the regulars show up on some preordained schedule. Miss Ruby, recently widowed six months back, has been a fixture at the bar for five months. I set her gin and tonic before her on a cocktail napkin. She sips it primly from the thin straw. Much to my annoyance Martin arrives and grunts out "the usual" as if anyone orders anything other than their usuals. His doe eyes follow me so closely one would think he is pining for my love but in truth he has one million things he wants to say to me particularly about Mandy and I do not want to hear a single fucking word. I slam his beer in front of him and loudly punch his order into the P.O.S. all without looking or speaking to him. This will continue until he leaves and fuels my hate fire by tipping me a ridiculous amount.

Cook finally gets to work to relieve the ladies. I make his drink of coke and grenadine with extra cherries, sweet enough to rot his teeth out of his head if they were not made of porcelain. He came with the name Cook, not because of his prowess in the kitchen, but because he used to be known for cooking meth. He spent years of his life in prison for it. Now the man is the poster child for the phrase "don't judge a book by its cover" with every inch of his skin covered in tattoos— mostly "insane clowns." Even his eyes, nose and mouth have forever been painted like one of his fellow posse members. After getting sober he has devoted his life to helping others to escape the throes of addiction and to seek out the path to recovery. When he is not here at work, he is leading meetings and helping those he's sponsored when they get out of jail or rehab. Cook is the "shirt off the back" type, atoning for past transgressions. He is the first to open his wallet if someone is in dire straights. He is genuinely one of the good ones.

"What are you doing later?" The voice makes me cringe. Peyton. Anyone this side of the Bible Belt has a twang that would be noticed elsewhere in the country, though some of the locals lean into the accent a little heavier than others like this guy. He is all Southern American drawl. Honey rich. The 'alright, alright, alright' type. From his broad face his teeth are just exposed bone, polished bright white. A wolf's smile flashed to anyone without a Y chromosome. That smile bespeaks his knowledge of the color of your bedspread from personal experience because like most of the women in this room, he has seen mine. Now, one would think with as much carnal experience as he has there would be something (anything) to make him and his prowess exceptional: size, stamina, acrobatics, hand puppets. But no. Blue-eyed, handsomeness, and no prejudices like race, religion, or in my case size, there is nothing special here.

He found me at my worst, my heart and self esteem in tatters, the aftermath of my first big break up. Almost immediately I regretted it. My sheets and comforter washed, bagged, and donated to Goodwill. Doctors' appointment scheduled for extra precaution despite all precautions already being taken. Peyton makes me sick and on occasion, like tonight I guess, he will insinuate we hang out (finger quotations), but I politely decline.

"None of your damn business," I spit out.

He chuckles as if to say, how cute, playing hard to get. "Hot date?"

I bat my thick lashes before answering, "Yep, with my toaster. In my bathtub."

He rolls his eyes but luckily just leaves me alone to find another victim.

It must be a bad day because Miss Ruby orders a third drink. But then upon closer inspection, I notice she is wearing make-up and dangling chandelier earrings. They swish back and forth with her movements and are much flashier than her usual style. "Want me to find you a ride home?" I ask.

She shakes her head. "I've got one," she blushes. Ah okay, she is getting a little loose tonight. Relieved by this I do not spare it another thought. I keep the drinks coming until midnight when we kick everyone out. There is only one fight, and it is in the parking lot which means it is not my problem, and the cops have already arrived. When my head hits my pillow, my work weary body instantly falls into sleep without worries since tomorrow is a mid shift, and I get to sleep in.

CHAPTER 4

"Your Vibe Attracts your Tribe"
motivational quote of the day

When I spy a painted wooden sign proclaiming "It's Fall Yall" I realize I am in my childhood living room. Instantly I look for my dad before filling with dread. The hospital bed is gone, and his well-loved recliner is back in its place. With trepidation I tip toe to the brown chair. Pain slices the soles of my feet. The floor is covered in eggshells. Blood seeps from my torn flesh leaving bright red footprints where I have been. Despite the pain I keep walking. The egg shards continue to rip me like broken glass until I finally reach the chair panting. I spin it around to see my dad is sitting in it, lifeless, his eyes milky white, his discolored skin pulled taut across his skull, limbs askew as their joints protrude from the emaciated frame. Movement under the cheek catches my attention. I follow its path to his open maw where antennas precede the segmented body of a centipede as it exits and scurries down the corpse. I try to scream but a sound like cracking ice heralds my mouth filling with fluid. This time when I open my jaw it is to retch and my teeth float out in a viscous river, bobbing up and down like little marshmallows in Swiss Miss.

I jump awake. Then fall back into my pillows, my hair damp at the temples. I take a minute to let my heartbeat settle to its normal speed. Dreams like this are fairly common for me so I will not spare it much thought but thanks to the adrenaline I guess I will not sleep in like I had hoped.

"You know you should be ashamed of these prices," the physical manifestation of a perfect plastic fashion doll says while loading two cartloads worth of shit onto the conveyor belt.

"You can send all complaints to corporate through our customer service department," I deadpan and gesture towards the area whose line is about ten deep.

"I wouldn't waste my time," she snaps back, all the while continuing to bitch about things I neither have nor want control over. *Ma'am, I make seventeen ninety-five an hour and you are hauling around a designer handbag whose repetition of initials over the sides are indicative of a price tag similar to a week of my pay.* I do not want her to have a nice day, but I say it anyway.

"I forgot to ring these up." She pries a bag of powdered donuts from her screaming child. I am about to say don't worry about it when the screaming child projectile vomits all over itself and the floor of my checkout line. I take a deep breath and resign myself to the fact that it is just going to be one of those days.

Indeed, it is. But thank Jesus, Buddha, Thor, fuck, whatever your preferred deity, the day goes fast, and I am now seated in a remote-controlled massage chair. My lower lumbar is getting pummeled on full blast by plastic fists and my tired toes are soaking in a mango scented whirlpool. Twice a month, my friends and I meet after hair and nail salon hours for pampering and gossip. Every single one of us is a "get-ready girl." The kind that someone with a weaker constitution would call "extra" or "high-maintenance." I am still waiting for an explanation as to why an individual who likes to look put together at all times is considered more work than someone who does not. I have my skin routine down to a fifteen-minute science thank you very much.

Tillie cuts the tips of my acrylic nails into coffin points while strips of her hair are bleaching blonde under tinfoil. Those money pieces are the only way to differentiate her from her sister Quinn. They move in a sync only those who share an exact genetic sequence can. They even finish each other's sentences, which was odd at first, but you get used to the way they operate.

"Faye had to clean up puke today," Dontae announces to the group, much to everyone's enjoyment, while Quinn is putting the finishing touches on his set of nails.

"Har Har. So funny," I reply.

Along with Dontae and the twins, Haven, a stylist at the salon, joins us. Her high pitch giggle is infectious and sets them off even further. Haven's name is perfect. She is angelic inside and out. Definitely the nicest out of all of us. Blue eyes, blonde ringlets, baby pink lips and cheeks. Even a smatter of light freckles decorates the bridge of her bubble gum nose. She expertly wields the tools of her trade, though being born with ectrodactyly. Her cleft hands are v-shaped with a thumb on one side and just one finger on the other. Tillie has painted all four of those nails a sky blue to match Haven's eyes.

There is a feast spread before us of expired bakery goods, an inexpensive premade charcuterie board, a jar of pickled okra and an untouched bag of baby carrots brought to have at least one healthy choice. The twins brewed a pot of green tea. As I take sips I look around at my friends. I would not have survived last year without this. Without them.

"All right, nails are done. I want to see my cards," Tillie says to Dontae who is already pulling out their tarot for some tips from the universe.

Haven looks to me, "He can start with them while I do your roots."

"Perf." I move closer.

"Are you still talking to Wyatt?" Haven asks shyly. The deepening of the pink on her cheeks makes me raise an eyebrow that was just waxed and tinted to maintain its villainous arch.

"No, nothing serious there. We just hung out a few times."

She does not say anything but nods while she works.

I hear Dontae snicker. I know how it sounds. I also know that if this were another time I would be treacherously close to spinsterhood at my age. But I do not know what I am looking for, only what I'm not.

"He's really nice," Haven says softly, while the rest of us share looks behind her back.

It's true, he is. They would make a great couple now that I think about it.

"Alright Queen you're up," our resident fortune teller says, and Haven pulls a card from his outstretched hands. She turns it to face us, her smile so big it rounds her cheeks. "Awwww shit, *The Lovers*." We all whoop and holler. There is some cat calling as well.

"Here you go creature of the night," Dontae jokes at me.

It's my turn. I pull a card I have never seen. "*Knight of cups?*"

"Hmmmm. This is interesting." He rubs his recently waxed chin in thought. The skin there smooth but reddish with irritation.

"What?!" Quinn yells and I agree what the hell.

"Faye, I believe you're going to meet your knight in shining armor, in the form of a dreamy young man."

This causes a riot of laughter and teasing but I do not believe it. I will not get my hopes up for anything anymore. If there is one lesson I have learned, it is hope is futile. Hope was all I had left, and I tried to keep it alive, but instead it starved, and I was left with nothing at all.

VIII
Strength

CHAPTER 5

Whatcha gonna Do when They come for You?

On Sunday mornings, like the good southern women they are, my mother and sister attend some meeting with other good southern Christian conservative ladies after church. I understand the timing makes me a coward, but this is my favorite time to visit my dad.

Only soft snores are heard as I enter the front door. One niece has curled her small body into my dad's side as they nap together. Dad calls this one his "little monkey" because she climbed before she walked. She is only three. Wistfully, I wonder if she will even remember him.

On the love seat is Kyle. He sleeps the deep sleep of someone with no worries. My other niece barely a year-old slumbers on his chest, her chubby hands fisting the straps of his thread bare tank top. His legs are too long for their makeshift bed, so his feet dangle over the edge of the cushions, the floppy slip-on man sandals on them dangling. I leave the bag of goodies in a spot they will see upon waking and quietly make my exit. I know I will be back tomorrow.

The week has drained me. I just want to make an entire sheet pan of loaded nachos and go to chow town. But when I pull into my designated parking spot there are two children there. My dark haired, dark eyed neighbors. The Little Shits, assigned Alex and Oscar at birth, are hovering around my steps and R.B. is making biscuits on the youngest of the two.

The brothers live in one side of the duplex approximately seventy-seven steps from my apartment which is eighteen wooden steps above a garage my landlord has packed full of junk. Once up the stairs there is a landing big enough for a cafe table with two matching wicker chairs and a couple of pots that I planted flowers in, but now only hold those plant's skeletal remains. A huge window is next to the red front door, in which a former resident put a cat door, much to my appreciation. (Though I bet they did not get their security deposit back.) The apartment itself is small but has a lot of natural light and there is a little patch of shared grass. It also has a window unit that in the throes of summer will turn my apartment into an ice box. I love the space and continually renew my lease. My landlord rewards my consecutive rental agreements by raising the cost three percent each contract.

"What's up nerds? Your mom working?" I ask when in range.

Alex continues to adore my cat, "Yeah, she told us not to bother you since it's your day off."

They are obviously not very good listeners since they are loitering in my designated area. "I was gonna make some nachos. You hungry?"

Their enthusiastic nods make me laugh. "I don't know why I asked, you're always hungry." I guess inflated grocery costs is one of the reasons their mom has to work so much. The boys follow me up the stairs, their short legs making the progress slower than mine, so I wait at the door. Both boys won the genetic lottery and were born with skeletal dysplasia, causing their legs and arms to be shorter than other kids their age. It has not stopped them from doing the things kids do, I had to step over their discarded bicycles to get to my steps.

"Can we do facials?" Oscar asks when he gets to the landing.

"You freaking know it," I answer. I unlock my door, and the brothers follow me inside.

Inside is an open floor plan. One half a kitchen, the other the living room space, separated by an island with two metal backed stools. The two doors on the adjacent wall lead you to a bedroom and a bathroom. Faces covered in mud, the three of us sprawl between my forest green couch and matching loveseat embellished with embroidered skeleton throw pillows and a blanket covered in bats I draped along the back. Horror and true crime filled bookshelves frame the tv on both sides, which we are watching a movie on. Among the spines sit knickknacks and potted pothos, their vines hang like tentacles towards the floor.

"There's a cop here," Alex yells as we all turn towards knocking at my front door.

"Distract him so I can go jump out the bathroom window," I answer.

The officer in question is rolling his eyes through that front window that I loved up until this moment. "I am literally making direct eye contact with you," he says before sighing, "no one's in trouble, I just want to talk to Faye," his words muffled by the glass.

Resignedly, I join him outside. "Howdy, Sheriff." One of the downsides to staying in the town you grew up in, is running into people you grew up with who also decided to stay in town.

I mock salute my former first love and recipient of my V card. Unfortunately, he is still all decadent shades of brown: eyes, skin, hair...toffee, caramel, chocolate. I send up a silent prayer to whatever God for the fact that he is in civilian clothing and not his uniform, while I stand here in leggings and an oversized shirt. At least I washed off the mud mask and my skin is gleaming.

"You look great," he says. Despite having one awful one-night stand, an awkward workplace affair and several years since he broke my heart, I still get a little shiver at the sound of his deep voice. That voice once told me he loved me and the foolish girl I was believed him. There is still a playlist in my collection dedicated to him aptly titled, "heartbreak induced rage mix."

"You look like you spend all of your free time at the gym." No sarcasm drips from my mouth, he is muscle on muscle. The Travis I knew was still pudgy in places. This version looks uncomfortably solid. Like a sidewalk.

"It's cheaper than therapy. I'm getting a divorce," he admits.

"Congratulations or condolences?" I reply awkwardly.

"Depends on who you ask..." he mumbles.

"So anyways...you're here, why?" I gesture towards one of the chairs and cross my fingers he does not fall right through it. They are a little weather worn. Just then a thought occurs to me. "Wait. Is there news?" I do not need to elaborate.

After Mandy's disappearance there were search parties full of volunteers. We went door to door with her missing flyer. There were social media blasts. A candlelight vigil was held on day four. I looked into the eyes of everyone attending to gauge how genuine their grief was. As the days slipped by with no leads, volunteers had to head back to their own lives, jobs, families, household chores. Hearing the words "there is nothing more we can do" is like a knife to the heart. It is a wound that will never fully heal, it festers without closure.

He scratches the back of his neck uncomfortably. "Sorry, no. I'm actually here to ask you a few questions about a different missing person's case." He takes out a black notepad so tiny that it looks stupid in his hands. Like he needed an X large, but they only had small.

Wait another missing person? "Who?"

"Did you work Wednesday night?" He asks, ready to get down to business.

"You know I did. You broke up the fight in the parking lot. It was karaoke night."

He nods and continues. "Was Miss Ruby there?"

"In her usual spot."

"Did you notice anything strange about her behavior?"

I take a moment to jog my memory. "It must have been a bad day; she had three gin and tonics. I asked her if she needed a ride, but she declined...she said she had one. She was dolled up that night. I think she may have had a date or was trying to find one."

He makes some notes, "Do you know who she left with?"

My stomach sinks. "No. I don't. It was crazier than usual. I poured just as many shots as drafts that night. Jenny Lee was there." I wish I had paid better attention.

"Now that's a one-woman party right there. She sing Gretchen or Shania?" Have to hand it to the regulars for being consistent.

"Both. I had a raging headache when I left." And selfishly gave no thought to how anyone was getting home other than myself.

"Damn. Did you see Miss Ruby talk to anyone? Who sat at the bar?" He scratches something down in his pad.

I tick off a bunch of names of more colorful locals. Travis knows every single one of them. "Martin..." I look him in the eyes as I say with gravitas. "Martin was there."

He sighs. "Not this again—you let your personal opinion cloud the truth," he argues.

"You let the fact that he was your football buddy influence what you know is the truth. His fingerprints were in Mandy's car. And he was at the bar on Wednesday, and I saw him talk to Miss Ruby," I reply harshly. If he were closer, I would be poking him in the chest to punctuate each word.

"Martin is a prick. He bullied you relentlessly in high school. Yes. But he's not a murderer. I wasn't the nicest to you either, but you don't hold the same grudge," he blushes a little.

"Says who?" I stare pointedly. I most definitely have not forgotten how he told me he had always had a crush on me since we sat next to each other in English twelfth grade. Or how he kept me like a dirty little secret for almost three whole years. (And stupid me I let him.) So not only did he put my heart in a blender and drink it like one of his after-workout protein shakes, but I also had to deal with the tatters of what little self confidence I had to begin with.

Travis sighs again dramatically. "I've already talked to him, and everything checks out." He pockets his notebook. "Faye I'm sorry," he tries.

I hold up my hand to stop him. It is my turn to say, "Not this again. I don't want to hear it." Luckily, Alex sticks his head out the door and saves me from this uncomfortable conversation.

"Faye the timer went off. Can I wash my face?" He is still wearing his mud mask.

"Yeah, bud, you know where the towels are. And clean up your damn mess." I can feel Travis watching me.

After Alex disappears back into my apartment Travis nods in that direction. "What's up with them?"

"My neighbor's. Their dad is in jail and their mom works non-freaking-stop. I try to help when I can by keeping an eye on them because she can't afford daycare or whatever it is you do with kids when you work."

"You watch them for free?" He has the audacity to make it sound almost condescending.

Fuck him. "Well yeah, they're super easy at this age. We play video games, eat snacks, do facials. You know, boy stuff."

He chuckles before turning to a more somber topic. "How's your dad?"

"Still dying." The words catch in my throat.

"I'm sorry," he says and I just shrug. What can I say—it is what it is, and I cannot change a thing.

"Want to grab dinner sometime?" he asks.

I look at him incredulously. *You have got to be kidding me.* "Please leave."

He flashes me a smile as he stands to go. "Figured it was worth a shot. See you around, Faye."

"Whatever," I mumble as I scramble to get away from him and memories I really, really do not want to dig up.

Interlude

Please excuse this brief interruption
before we continue our regularly scheduled program.

Interviewer: We're here today to discuss the disappearance of thirty-year-old Mandy Harris. Joining us today is Mandy's best friend Faye Denton. Thank you for talking to us under the circumstances. Do you remember anything about the day you first discovered Mandy was missing?

Faye: Of course. Every single detail. We both had mid-shifts that day. I texted her to see if she wanted a coffee because at first I thought she was just running late. After thirty minutes, when we were due to clock in, I tried calling her thinking maybe her alarm didn't go off. Nothing. It's not like her to "no call, no show," so I went to her parent's house after work.

Interviewer: Why'd you go to her parent's house?

Faye: Oh, she had moved back home to save money. Her mom answered the door and seemed as surprised as me to find Mandy wasn't there even though her car was in the driveway. On her passenger seat was her purse and phone. There weren't any obvious signs of struggle or anything...no blood. Excuse me. (Blows nose in tissue.)

Interviewer: What happened next?

Faye: One of the guys we went to high school with is now a Sheriff. I went to him. We used to be close. I thought he'd help me. I filed the missing persons report right away. It's not like the movies, you don't have to wait 48 hours. There was so much action at first. They went door to door asking questions, combed her social media, there were organized search parties for any patch of land with more than a few trees. And then as each day passed with no new information, it just fizzled out.

Interviewer: *Was there any kind of evidence at all?*

Faye: *They found fingerprints in her car. The cops said that after talking with the person who left them, he wasn't a suspect.*

Interviewer: *You sound like you don't agree.*

Faye: *I don't.*

Interviewer: *Why is that?*

Faye: *The fingerprints in her car belonged to someone we hated: Martin Holmes.*

Interviewer: *Sheriff Travis Avery told us in his interview that Mandy was in a romantic relationship with Martin Holmes.*

Faye: *(Getting agitated) I know what Travis thinks. But Mandy wouldn't...*

Interviewer: *Do you think Mandy didn't tell you about their relationship because she knows how you personally feel about him?*

Faye: *No. Well, at least I don't think so.*

CHAPTER 6

True Crime Ruined my Life
. . . now streaming

"You're disgusting!" "She's got more hair on her face than you do, man!" A tomato smashes into my chest, the guts burst into a seedy mess. Among the hecklers are faces I know. Travis and Martin. My mother and sister. They spit hateful words and actual mucus to me as I run through the crowd. Tears stream down my face and dampen the beard that has grown over my cheeks and chin in dark waves. "Run away, you freak!" they scream. And I do. My tennis shoes slap against the familiar asphalt of the streets I used to ride my bike on. My heart pounds until I round a corner and see a large red and white striped tent erected in the ballfield. It is lit with strung lights and the yellow glow calls to me like a beacon. A safe haven. I pump my chubby legs as fast as they will go, practically diving through the thick canvas flaps. Someone stands in the center of the ring in a top hat, their back to me as they say in a voice I recognize but cannot at the moment place. "All are welcome here."

I wake to the rain pounding the worn shingles on my roof. I have not had a bearded lady dream in quite a while. I guess I can thank yesterday's trip down memory lane for that. It was not long after I went to the doctor for the hair growing on my face and chest that I was diagnosed with Poly Cystic Ovarian Syndrome and Travis dumped me. Good times. I am lying, it was not good times.

Gutters that have not been cleaned of their detritus spew water over the sides. As I become more aware, is my bed wet? Is my ceiling leaking? Did the rushing gutter waterfall make me pee the bed? I pat around me, there is something damp. I throw back my covers to discover the source and bite back a groan. Bright red blood covers my lower half, the sleep shorts I wore were no match for the force of Mother Nature and I look like I was hacked at night by an eight-inch butcher knife. White hot pain slices though my abdomen, not phantom pains but actual cramps. Thankfully, the big corporate powers that be grant us sick days. Today, I will be using one.

After a shower so hot I am surprised I still have flesh over my bones, I change my bed sheets. While I am fortunate enough to have a washer and dryer, stacked into one exceedingly small yet apartment friendly appliance, my comforter will not fit. I rinse it out in the tub since I will not be leaving my sanctuary today, especially not for the laundromat. No today I am using my heated blanket like a tortilla and wrapping myself into a human burrito while I watch murder shows and reality television. Yes my happy place may seem a tad dull but a) I have not been murdered, b) I am not morbidly obese, c) I am not currently surrounded by a hoard of trash and d) I do not have an entire horn growing out of my head that makes me depressed and self conscious, yet I have let grow for fifty years, until a television show offers to pay to get it removed. Sometimes all you need is a little perspective. On one hand comparison is the thief of joy, on the other it gifts appreciation. Circling back to perspective.

Corporate gave me some time off and my insurance agreed to pay for six virtual therapy sessions to help cope with the trauma of losing my best friend. This work-approved psychiatrist encouraged me to find comfort in my day-to-day motions and routines. Aka get back to work. I mean it was inevitable that I would have to since I did not want to starve and there was no way in hell I was moving back to my parents. The deadline to wellness was only exacerbated by the oncoming holidays. I had to be healed by holiday launch which was a week earlier than the year prior. The chaos that is retail work preceding Santa Claus rolling into town with baby Jesus riding shotgun is like nothing else. The cherry on top is the flux of seasonal drinkers. Having to deal with obligatory family interactions or not having family to deal with, either way it seems alcohol is the preferred coping mechanism. And then my dad got sick and sicker fast. It did seem like that therapist was right, all the noise in my life shushed the voice in my head that repeatedly said things like "How can you go on like nothing happened?"

But of course, I was not unscathed. I have always been a lucid dreamer but in the early days of Mandy's disappearance, I could not sleep at all. Any time I closed my eyes I pictured every horrible thing that has ever been done to a woman being done to her. True crime documentaries fueled my imagination fire so

I could not stomach watching them. But that changed when I became an armchair investigator and began to watch them for educational purposes. Maybe there will be something in one of these cases that by happenstance yields some kind of a clue. Wishful thinking on my part but one thing that is repeatedly said by law enforcement is that there are no coincidences, and it only takes one line to start connecting dots.

Steaming bowl of ramen in my lap, I lay on my couch, feeling about as good as I am going to. R.B. presses into my thigh as close as he can get without sitting in my food. I drape noodles over the bowl's sides so they reach room temperature, and he can share my lunch. This is the two dollars for one type, not the two dollars for six. The kind of ramen you eat because you want to, not because you have to, though some days are thin enough that I have to as well.

Despite being literally found in a dumpster, the dumpster at "The Hole" to be exact, R.B. can be a picky little prince when he wants to. My cat looks up at me with his glowing orange eyes as if to say "thank you, but you know I prefer the shrimp flavor." Everything about him is orange except the white tips of his toes and tail. A more rational human would have named him something like "Pumpkin Spice," but my middle name is not Rational it is Marie after a great, great grandmother I never met.

Unsurprisingly, the detective on my television screen is talking about coincidences right now in relation to the case that is being covered. "We reached out to neighboring counties to inquire about any missing girls and realized they all had open investigations." My ears perk at that. Had my own local investigators done that very thing? Why hadn't I? I scare R.B. off my lap with sudden movement as I jump forward to get my phone from the coffee table. I instantly start searching and what I find turns my blood to a gas station slushee.

CHAPTER 7

34.18058 N, 80.31362 W

It goes without saying, though I am mentioning it anyways, adulthood can be monotonous. Lorded over by time: schedules, appointments, etc. When the boredom becomes too much, we do something to change our current narrative; take a fitness class, learn the pottery wheel, cut our hair, or start a docuseries. Or those feeling extra dramatic will get married, get divorced, make a baby, or adopt a dog, maybe take out a large loan—or perhaps find themselves walking down a footpath around Scape Ore Swamp on a hunch—like I am doing at 11:34 on a Sunday afternoon.

This is it. I have officially lost all of my marbles. After checking in with Dad I drive thirty-six minutes and one county over to trudge around in woefully inadequate footwear because of a gut feeling, a momentary intuitive thought. I park my car in the grass on the side of the road and take the path leading down a hill and just past the bridge, in hopes the murky black water will bubble up secrets like the little triangle in a Magic Eight ball. So far, it is just a swamp, like any other swamp around here, of which there are many.

Cypress trees poke out of the water with their knobby knees gathered around them. Spanish moss hangs limply from the limbs in stringy green-gray tendrils. Palmetto leaves grow out in large fans from the ground like peacock tails. Birds chirp and squawk, a woodpecker drums nearby and the bugs are fucking ruthless. They buzz and screech and land on you no matter how much deterrent spray you apply because it is so hot and humid you sweat your protection right off.

If we are talking seasons, it is technically Fall, but the temperatures are still rising to the eighties. The humidity weighs down the air, I can feel it all around me like I am moving through sludge. Any stray tendril of hair that has fallen out of my bun is plastered to my neck and forehead similar to the creeping vines in this very environment. My eyelashes clump together with every blink despite only having one application of mascara.

As I bob down the path guzzling water from my thermos, light reflects off two green slitted eyes that watch me from the camouflage of the plants on the water's surface. I have a vague recollection of taking a field trip to one of these swamp areas and I am sure I learned those plant's names, but I do not remember, nor do I really care. I am a little worried the pocketknife I brought probably will not be a match for the alligator if it decides to spring. I pick up the pace, again with no actual agenda in mind.

I am an indoor girl through and through, though this place is not completely foreign to me. Mandy and I have been to the festival celebrating the local celebrity, the Lizardman. We drank green-dyed lemonade and bought human-shaped reptilian dolls crocheted by cute grannies. There was a parade and a car show, it was all good small-town fun. But never had I once had the desire to stomp through the actual swamp until now when some invisible force is pulling me here. This blue squiggle on a map in between counties where at least six women are unaccounted for. While amateur sleuthing and correlating my findings, the location of Scape Ore just poked and prodded me until all I could think of was at least coming here and seeing it with my own eyes. And now that I am here,

I cannot suppress my shiver, this place gives me the creeps. And it stinks like eggs and trash.

My tennis shoes continue to sink into the soft earth. I have my eyes glued to the ground, aware of each step, because I am convinced every bare limb is a snake. I am hyper aware of any leaf rustle, again questioning my so-called intuition. Another shudder goes down my spine wondering what creatures could be watching me, so of course I walk right through a spider web. Ghost legs crawl all over my skin. "Ugh." I suppress a gag.

I make it to a place where a cypress tree has ripped from the ground and fallen into the water. A dragonfly flits around me and then lands on its bark. That weird feeling that the universe is guiding me settles into my gut, so I take a minute and sit on the makeshift bench. The rough bark digs into my backside as I toe the swamp's shore, black coffee dark water lapping it. Something grabs my shoe, and I have only an instant to pull my foot back before the bumpy moss-covered head of a snapping turtle surfaces, trying to bite me. The speed at which I jerk back almost makes me tumble off the tree. The turtle opens his pointed beak to hiss at me. "Fuck you too!" I shout, breathlessly. Heart now beating at erratic speeds, I decide I have had enough nature for one day and high tail it back to my car for air conditioning and contemplation.

CHAPTER 8

Active Ingredient: DEET

A week of life distractions and obligations, hours clocked, and time with my dad has passed and I find myself inexplicably back at Scape Ore. I have been in my head all week, but if any of my friends noticed, they were too preoccupied with their own bullshit to say anything.

I park my car on the side of the road in the same spot as last time, but unlike last time I have on rubber boots that I purchased yesterday from work with my employee discount. Before starting the trail, I apply a fresh coat of bug spray, one already applied in my driveway. Little winged bodies ping pong off my exposed skin. I swallow down my repulsion and steel myself for another walk through this hellscape as I descend the hill, all the while wondering why people find hiking enjoyable.

"Hey! You shouldn't go out there by yourself," a voice calls to me from up the embankment. I instantly pull out my pocketknife. The snick it makes when opening practically echoes in the air between me and this stranger. The figure is backlit so I cannot see any of his features except that he is tall and lanky with unkempt hair and black framed glasses. He holds up his hands in surrender. "I'm not trying to start trouble. I just figured since you're obviously not from here you should know there are alligators. There have also been a few cougar sightings and black bear have been spotted here too. And poisonous snakes," he rambles.

"Are we really playing 'man or bear' right now?" I raise a perfectly arched eyebrow and hold up my weapon.

He is still far enough away that I cannot clearly see him, but I hear his huff of amusement. "Look if you're going monster hunting just know you'll find something more real and more dangerous. That's all I'm saying."

"I'm not monster hunting," I throw out, unsure of why I feel the need to defend myself. While also not wanting a stranger to know where I am going. And that I am going alone, even though that is obvious.

"Yeah okay. Sure," he replies sarcastically.

I look down at myself and I have on a shirt that says "Monster Lover" with cartoon creature heads. Okay, I look the part. "I swear I'm not."

"Then why are you hiking here? There's a nice park less than twenty minutes away," he replies in exasperation.

"I don't know," I admit. Then turn around and leave, not feeling particularly threatened anymore. I do not get a gut feeling of wrongness from him, my hackles do not raise, no fight or flight response and I have a good fifty pounds on the guy. And a knife. Besides sweat is already beading on my upper lip and raining from my boobs like some meditative water feature. I need to get going. I walk away.

I make it to the same spot where the natural cypress tree bench is. I sit on the trunk and again look out into the murky depths. Once more I am left with the questions, why am I here and what do I hope to find? Then like it is playing on loop a dragonfly zips around me before landing on the tree as well. I would take it as a sign from Mandy, but she hates bugs more than I do.

If she were going to send me a message, she would do it with something fuzzy and cute, like a panda. She loves pandas.

Every twig snap, crunch of debris, and water gurgle or splash has me jumping thanks to the "Good Samaritan." I am too twitchy to sit here more than a few minutes, my imagination running wild with animal attack scenarios. With a "fuck this" I trudge back.

Tucked in the shadow of the bridge I see the do-good stranger is still here. Apprehension makes me pause, until I get close to see he is reading a comic, and I am not sure why, but that puts me at ease, so I do not even pull my blade this time.

"What are you doing?" I ask, not hiding the irritation in my voice because, really, what is he doing?

"Waiting to make sure you weren't eaten by swamp animals," he replies dryly from behind the cover he is holding.

"Why?" I ask as I try to get close enough to really see him.

He shuffles further into the patch of dark. His baggy clothing in black and gray, make it impossible to see anything other than general shapes. Even his voice is vague, not deep or high, so I cannot gauge how old he is either. "I don't know. Didn't want it on my conscience I guess."

"Umm, okay, but aren't you being eaten alive by bugs?" I ask.

"Nah, I live around here. I always carry bug spray." He is still behind his book like a shield.

I should just move along and ignore him, but I cannot help myself (chalking this up to boredom again) and continue to engage in conversation. "I still don't understand why you waited. What are you, some kind of weirdo?"

"Maybe. Depends on who you ask," he shrugs.

A laugh bubbles out of me at his self deprecation. As I get closer, details of Mr. Weirdo finally become clearer, and he starts to get visibly discomfited under my scrutiny. "You're all right. I guess I'll go now," he mumbles and scurries to leave, his checkered slip-ons slipping on the wet ground. My brain tries to catch up with what I saw. That could not be right though. From what I could make out, as he left in a hurry, it looked like his tan skin was covered in scales.

CHAPTER 9

First Sighted in 1988

I taste a scent on the current. The aroma catches my attention as I glide through the cloudy water. I navigate a maze of grasses and tree roots as my legs paddle towards it following an instinct passed down to me from my ancestors, large terrifying beasts, my claws, my beak, a fraction of their power. A tangle of yellow strands floats towards the surface where I will need to go soon for air. But for now my thoughts are only the scent and tasting the flesh before me. In excitement, hunger gnaws my belly. For a moment I pause. A glint of gold floats around my meal. A memory sparks. A misplaced halo. In the dark it is hard to see the details though I strain my beady eyes. Get closer. A little gold bear attached to the chain winks back at me. My knotty head jerks back. Through the bubbles I make when I scream, I recognize a face. Even though it is mottled gray and blue and waxy with swampy bloat.

My body jolts as I surface, gasping for air. My skin is damp with sweat like the residual water from the cold depths I was just swimming. The necklace in my dream looked an awful lot like the one I gifted Mandy three years ago for Christmas.

Alright Faye, you need another virtual psychiatric evaluation. Restless energy zips through my limbs fueling me to continue what has become my day-off routine of encasing myself in protective chemicals before taking the trail to the felled cypress wearing a jack o' lantern shaped backpack that holds my massive water bottle. Anticipation takes me hastily back to the bridge. My ponytail swings back and forth like a pendulum as I walk.

My pulse pounds as I get closer, and the very person I want to interrogate is there skipping rocks over the water's surface. "You came back." He shakes his head in a visible 'tsk tsk' motion, although it seems he was hoping I would. He is wearing some video game shirt, and I now see that his shaggy hair has an auburn tint in the one sun beam that has pierced the tree canopy. He wears it long enough to curl over his forehead and ears obscuring his face, because like I thought he is covered in patches of scaly skin. These patches are a little darker than his skin tone. The same color as the iced coffee the twins make. The scales cover his cheeks and run along the sides of neck. Down his forearms to his hands, which are particularly bad around the knuckles. At my scrutiny, he tucks them into the pockets of his black jeans. "Why?" he asks in exasperation.

"Because I have questions," I state. I had a constant ache for days like a bad tooth. Until it occurred to me one day this week that if this guy is a local, there is a possibility he has witnessed something out of the ordinary. Or it is possible that he will even recognize my friend.

"Um, okay," he says shyly, clearly caught off guard.

"Have you seen any weird activity or strange cars? Anything that made you pause…?" I plow on.

He gives me a pointed look before answering jokingly, "Other than you and the toaster on wheels with the bumper sticker that says, 'My other ride is a decaying flesh sack'?"

Whatever, I love my car.

"Haha. But seriously, do you recognize this person?" I get close enough to show him pictures of Mandy on my phone. He has more than a few inches over my height, so he must lean down to get a better look. I catch the scent of citronella now that we stand together. That natural stuff is not strong enough to keep bloodsuckers at bay for me. I must have type O.

A moment passes before he answers, "I have never seen her. I'm sorry." This close I see his eyes are a vivid green behind his heavy framed spectacles. I did not have any expectations, but I still get a twang of disappointment.

"Who is she?" he asks gently, eyes softening.

"My best friend. She's been missing for almost a year," the words heavier in the thick air between us.

"Wait," he berates me, "your best friend is missing, and you've been hiking alone. Don't you think that's a little reckless?"

"I have protection," I answer.

"Oh, that's right, a pocketknife."

Who the hell does he think he is?

"And bear spray, now that someone told me there are bears out here." Yes, I do have the audacity to harumph after this statement. "And heft. Fat people are harder to kidnap." I put my hands on my round hips, which are accentuated in the black leggings I am wearing, to emphasize how hard it would be to drag me anywhere I did not want to go.

He slides a hand down his face before replying, "You are not fat." He is looking anywhere but directly at me. His cheeks darken. He quickly changes the subject. "So you're here, what, looking for clues?"

"Yes." *Duh.*

Movement under his hair implies a brow lift, though I cannot see them under the reddish waves. "Why here exactly?"

"Intuition." The only answer I truly have for my antics.

He has a moment of speculation. "Am I a suspect?"

My head whips back. "No."

"Shouldn't I be?" he asks, and worries his bottom lip with his teeth.

Is he serious right now? "You don't fit the profile."

He laughs loudly. "What could possibly make you qualified to make that judgement call?"

"True crime novice."

He is not impressed with my answer.

"Okay, most missing people are found. The percent of those not is really low, like one or two percent. So, the odds something really bad happened, I have to accept, are pretty high. Most people who have been..." I almost choke on the next word, it lodges in my throat, "...murdered...know the person who did it." I take a deep breath to steady myself and ignore his sympathy. If he were a psychopath, he would not have that look on his face. Or he is, and therefore very good at mimicking human emotions. "What would be your motive?"

"I was bullied," he answers, "and desensitized by violent games."

"Everyone was bullied. Try harder," I challenge.

"Bullies don't get bullied," he states matter of factly.

"Yes they do. Probably by their parents. That's why they pick on someone else. What about a head injury when you were a baby?" I grip my chin in contemplation.

"I don't think so?" His face scrunches in confusion.

"What about sports?" I continue. "You play any full contact football?"

"Some Little League baseball, but I mostly kept the bench warm." He holds his hands out in surrender.

"Do you have a tendency to start fires?" I continue my scrutiny.

He looks perplexed but humors me with an answer. "No."

"How about chronic bed wetting?" I really have no filter.

At this he looks positively horrified, "Definitely no, and also none of your business. Do these specific questions have some sort of meaning to you?"

"Animal cruelty?" The train of thought I am on keeps on chugging.

"I don't even eat red meat, again what does this have to do with me being a suspect?" He clearly does not watch Dateline or 20/20.

"The MacDonald triad... it has been linked to future violent offenders. So, nope. You? Not a suspect."

"Man, you're weird." He smiles when he says it, so I do not take offense.

"Besides, I can't picture you doing a nefarious deed in checkered slip-ons. Maybe if you had on, like, big boots or something. And didn't wear those hipster glasses. You'd need the metal ones; they sell them at the Halloween store and call them serial killer glasses since they were a popular look with murderers back in the day." I use my fingers to air quote. "And the Emo bangs. There's not much threatening about you. Sorry. You have a dragon on your shirt, for God's sake."

"Thank you, I'll take all that as a compliment." He smiles again and it is an honest to goodness smile showing his straight teeth and dimples. Poor guy, he is pretty cute under all that thick scaly skin.

Unbridled, a ridiculous thought races to the front of my mind.

"Oh my God, are you Lizardman?" I practically squeal.

He rolls his eyes, "No, that's my Granddad." He holds up his hands before I ask more. "And no, I won't elaborate. That's his story to tell."

"So you're Lizard Boy?" I ask, delighted.

He chuckles before answering. "This is Ichthyosis Vulgaris, fish scale syndrome. If anything, I'm Fish Boy."

I snicker. "Fish Boy connotes a certain smell." I wrinkle my nose.

He makes a face as well. "Okay, Lizard Boy it is then, or you could just call me Marcus," he says shyly, almost boyishly, while scratching the back of his neck.

"I'm Faye," I reply without hesitation.

"Um, cool. Yeah, so if you, you know...come back next week...you know...I can come with you if you want. To help look for clues, or watch your back."

I wonder if he has had much social interaction, because he sure can ramble a lot when he feels awkward.

"It seems like you're here anyways. So sure," I tease.

"Sunday, I get my grocery pick up. Lizardman makes me buy things like sardines in mustard, and pickled beets. I can not buy those in person. I drive right by here to go home."

"But when will you pick up your groceries if you're swamp frolicking?" I ask playfully. Not flirting. I am not flirting. I am a grown-ass woman; we do not flirt.

"Saturday," he answers. "I'll just have to schedule it around my gaming schedule. I'm in a zoom campaign."

And then at that moment some frozen piece of me instantly thaws, knowing Marcus is a giant nerd and that means we could be friends. But why that makes me so happy I decide it is better to not analyze and do what I do best: put it away for later.

CHAPTER 10

Google, What's that Romeo in Black Jeans Song?

It is funny how long a week can drag out when you have something you are looking forward to. How time stretches itself out like taffy. Though we are not putting the reason for my excitement under scrutiny, it is monotony not loneliness that fuels us. And then the moment you have been looking forward to is here and you are parking your sticker adorned toaster on wheels behind a generic gray/silver two door sedan.

Leaning on the hood, Marcus barely nods to acknowledge my presence because his attention is solely on his phone. He holds it horizontally while his thumbs furiously control the little character in his game.

I tilt my head for a better view. "There's a bonus level in that cave, you can collect a shit-ton of coins," I advise.

He gives me a brief glance before deciding to trust me. I am proven right as he racks up a bunch of points before saving his progress. After pocketing his phone, he looks to me with big puppy-dog eyes. No those are Christmas morning eyes. All surprise and awe and "hmmm what do we have here" excitement. I make a noncommittal shrug. "You coming or what?" Then I head toward my thrice taken foot path.

As Marcus excitedly details the game he is playing, I watch how he skips around, his hair bounces with each step. I am struck with the thought again just how boyish he is and that he emanates this golden retriever-like energy. If he had a tail, I swear it would be wagging right now. He is wearing his preferred laceless black-and-white canvas shoes, thin athletic pants, and an anime shirt. He stops mid-stride in a wider spot on the trail to let me pass and take the lead, then changes the topic. "I really like your tattoos, I've always wanted them but I'm not sure how'd they heal with my skin." I recognize his rambling is a strategy he uses when nervous. I have a feeling he is much younger than me, not that I am an old maid or anything, but I also do not want to play the role of "Maude."

"Marcus how old are you?" I give voice my to my growing concern.

"Twenty-six," he replies, from where he now follows behind me.

Just as I thought. I groan. "I graduated before you even went into high school."

"How is that even relevant now that we're both grown ups with jobs and taxes and whatnot?" He asks and I can admit he does have a point, I guess.

"You're not going to ask me how old I am?" I throw the question behind me.

"No—Faye what exactly do you have planned? I thought we were just taking a trail," he says in mock horror.

"I'm 31." I just have to say it. In fact, it practically falls out of my mouth.

"When is your birthday?" Marcus asks.

"October 30th." Yes, I am a Scorpio Queen.

"Explains a lot," he says sarcastically in reference to my pumpkin shaped backpack, skeleton printed leggings and black everything else. (Braid, nails, eyeliner, soul.)

"I think I would have loved Halloween regardless. It's always been my favorite," I admit.

"It's definitely my favorite, too." His reply makes me glance behind and when he catches my look, his mouth ticks up in a crooked smile. I trip over a root and quickly face forward again.

"You have a job?" As soon as I ask this question, I realize how dumb it sounds.

"Well, yeah, how else do people afford life," he answers my ridiculous question with snark, and I respect him more for it.

"Ha. Ha. Well, okay smarty what do you do?" We have arrived at what I now call MY cypress tree, and I turn to face him. Behind his glasses, his eyes match the background foliage.

"You know how schools had to give kids all those laptops when they went virtual during the pandemic?" He asks while gripping the straps of the backpack he carries to hold his bug repellent and water bottle.

"Yeah, I guess. I don't have any kids so I didn't pay that much attention. My job never shut down either, so I just kept on trucking through it all," I answer honestly.

"Well, I'm one of the county's I.T. guys. I fix all the broken computers and network bugs. I had just started when all that happened. It was madness. I got a lot of hate mail."

That makes me snort. Of course he is a computer guy.

"What about you?" he asks.

"I work retail during the day and then three nights a week I bartend," I reply. The rough bark of the tree presses into my thighs as I sit. I tuck a stray hair that has come out of its elastic band behind my ear.

"Are you going to school? What do you want to do?" He asks and I have never had a "poker face" so it is obvious his question strikes a nerve.

"Nothing Marcus. I don't want to do anything. Why can't I work a register forever?" I ask a tad more aggressively than I mean to.

He holds up his hands, "I didn't mean to offend you."

"I don't need a degree because there's nothing I want to go to school for. It would literally be a glorified piece of paper. I don't need a fancy job title to feel important. My job is just so I can have money. I don't have a life's purpose, or a dream or a goal. I have a cute apartment, I obviously dote on myself." I wave my manicured hands to show off my long, pointed nails, "I buy myself little treats all of the time...isn't that successful? I don't have this desire to feel special. Isn't it enough to find a few people who think I'm special and leave it at that?"

"I'm sorry Faye. I didn't mean to sound like a dick." He looks at me so bashful I sigh. I feel like I kicked him.

"It's okay. I get asked that a lot actually. I'm sorry I got all heated," I apologize. "Even in elementary school I didn't know what I wanted to be when I grew up. All I could think of was *not bored*."

He looks up as he recalls his own memories. "Mine always changed...first it was a train conductor...then I wanted to be a marine biologist in my dolphin phase."

I do not say anything, but I must make a face.

"What? Every kid has a dolphin phase," he defends himself.

"They definitely don't," I reply dryly. "Speaking from experience."

"Okay fine. But I grew out of it when my dad wouldn't let me wear the dolphin shirt I got on a field trip to the aquarium. He said it was girly, but dolphins are clearly gender fluid."

"I'll agree with you on that one," I nod emphatically.

He changes the subject. "So, where's your apartment?"

"In the same town I grew up in. Let me guess you have thoughts on that, too?" He starts to say something, but I just barrel on like a wrecking ball. "Why don't I move somewhere else, right? Like it's so easy to come up with first month's and second month's rent for a security deposit. Plus a pet deposit and other made-up fees these landlords lord over us. Don't forget utility deposits and paying for a moving truck..." I trail off.

"I'm pretty lucky I haven't had to really deal with that, He says shyly. "I went from home, to college, to living with a roommate, to where I am now."

I do not begrudge anyone for living with a parent, even Mandy moved back home to save money. Her parents are not the worst, but they are not the best either. They are the type that will say, "we're not racist..." and then go on to say something really fucking racist. I realize with a start that this could be another reason Mandy was keeping her relationship with Martin a secret, her awful parents.

"Do you live alone, or do you have a roommate?" Marcus asks, and I am thankful he has interrupted my current revelation.

I laugh at his question. "You're not gonna catch much with the way you're fishing," I joke before putting him out of his misery. "It's just me and my cat, R.B."

It is not my imagination, he visibly relaxes. "I took you for a dog person."

I bristle. "Oh no. Haven't you heard of the Son of Sam? The dog possessed by an ancient demon that told his neighbor to murder?"

"Uhhh, I don't think so." He gives a funny look. "Are you saying Arby, or the letters R and B?"

"R and B," I reply.

He cocks his head to the side, "What does it stand for?"

I swat away a dragonfly zooming around my head. "Rat Bastard."

"You named your cat Rat Bastard?" he asks, clearly amused.

"Yes. I was taking out the trash at "The Hole"...that's the bar I work at, and something flew out at me from the dumpster. At first I thought it was a rat, so I was like 'aaah a rat!' But then I realized it was a kitten covered in chocolate syrup, so I started murmuring sweet nothings to him. Then the bastard bit me. So that's how he got his name."

Marcus is laughing at me, "You are kind of ridiculous. You know that, right?"

I do not answer him.

He lowers himself on to the tree next to me. We both sit quietly for a moment looking out over the still water. There is something peaceful about it all. Well, I am looking out at the water, Marcus is looking at me. His ogling has me a little self conscience, I know I am encased in a sheen of sweat and though I am wearing my preferred color black, I have dark pit stains. "What?"

He shakes his head before answering, "I've been to this spot before."

"Oh, you've brought another girl here before?" Now who's fishing?

I glimpse a dimple as he says, "Didn't you...bring me here?" He muses, "Besides, it's hard to get girls to go anywhere with you when you're ugly."

My heart breaks a little for him even though we just met. "You're not ugly." I realize I mean it. Once you get over that first glimpse of his skin condition, you hardly notice it. "If you're Fish Boy, I'm the Bearded Lady," I say gently.

He looks over my entire face. "What do you mean?"

I am thankful for my full coverage foundation, liquid concealer, and expensive setting spray at this moment in time. Otherwise, my blush would be evident.

"I have to dermaplane my face every morning with this little pink plastic razor. That's just a fancy word for lady shaving. If I didn't, I would grow a full beard. Ichthyosis Vulgaris, meet Hirsutism. If we joined a circus we'd be the stars of the show."

He beams at me, "You'd certainly be the Belle of the Ball."

"I'd insist on a trio of very normal, very average looking ladies to wait on me. They'd have to assist me with my daily baths in oat milk and rose petals. My beard would have to be brushed and treated with exotic oils to keep it lush and shiny like a mink pelt." I exaggerate my extraness with arm gestures for Marcus' amusement.

"Don't forget your nails," he teases. "You'd have to keep them long and sharp to fend off all of your fans."

"That is how I like them," I say wistfully.

"Didn't I tell you cougars had been sighted in this swamp?" his laughter erupts.

"That's it, I'm pushing you in the water." My statement only brings him more merriment before he lurches away from me.

On the walk back I barely notice the dragonfly flying around my head, it is as light and delicate as my mood right now.

VI
The Lovers

CHAPTER 11

Ch-ch-changes

"Can I see what shades of green you have?" My question is like a record scratch, all conversation stops, and every head turns in my direction. Tillie comes to a halt mid-manicure, Dontae swivels so we are facing, Quinn pauses her work on Dontae's own nail set, and Haven lifts her head from digging the chocolate pieces out of our store brand trail mix.

"What?" I ask in defense. "I'm feeling like a little change." They accept my answer, and we all carry on.

While Tillie is brushing the mossy green I have chosen onto my fingertips, Dontae clears his throat. "I guess since 'Miss Black Is the Color of my Soul' is feeling a little change, I guess it's time to announce my own." He takes a deep breath while we all wait to hear the news. "I've been talking to a store in Richmond about transferring."

"Virginia?" I squeak.

"Yep," he answers. Quinn grunts all the while using a single strand paint brush to make little flowers the size of rice grains on Dontae's acrylic set.

"Why do you want to move?" Haven voices what we are all wondering.

"Because, I'm tired of sneaking off with closeted boys. I don't want to be the only loud and proud queer around. I'd like to settle down. His and his hand towels, matching pajama nondenominational holiday cards. Can't you picture me sipping mimosas at drag brunch cooked by a chef covered in tattoos of vegetables...not clowns. There are whole communities of me..." he trails off.

My heart breaks a little because I want that for him so bad and I feel like a terrible friend for not realizing he should have had that sooner. Leaving small town life and smaller minds behind.

"I was going to go sooner. I haven't left yet because of..." Dontae does not have to say it we all know he did not leave because of Mandy and...well, me. He is looking directly at me now, his eyes glassy. His unspoken words shining in them, he has not moved yet because I was hanging on by a fucking thread. He is such a good friend and I feel awful and selfish.

"I want you to go." I cannot hide the waiver in my voice. "But make sure your couch is big enough for plus size visitors," I say with as much gusto as I can. He nods. There is too much emotion in the room.

Dontae pulls a card slowly from his tarot deck on the counter, mindful of his drying polish. It is the six of swords. A figure on a raft is floating off into the distance. "I've pulled this card over and over again. I know I need to go. I'll miss you all... but I need this."

We offer our murmurs of understanding and encouragement. "Faye, wanna see what the stars have in mind for you?"

"No, I think I'm going to let it be a surprise." And I mean it.

It is finally my lunch break. For the past hour I have been fantasizing about the turkey sandwich I packed. I even have a side Tupperware of pickles to slip between the slices of jalapeño cheese bread I splurged on. I am almost to the break room door when I see her, a teenage girl shoving rolled jeans into her hoodie. I close my eyes and heave a sigh. I do not have the time nor the patience for this shit.

"Hey," I announce my presence to the girl who is maybe sixteen. Whatever her actual age, her frontal lobe is clearly not developed yet. She stops—deer in the headlights style. "So, listen...a little advice. There are cameras everywhere, and Bill...he's head of loss prevention...he's watching all of them from a little room up front. Odds are he already has seen you, but if you put everything back, I'm sure he'll leave you be. And I won't have to fill out an incident report. Everyone is cool. You won't have this slip in judgement forever on your record."

She continues to stare at me, unblinking, I wonder if she thinks she has gone invisible. I do not know. I have a date with a turkey sandwich, so I continue my trek to the break room.

Someone has microwaved something that has left an unfortunate smell lingering in the air. No bother, I am practically starving, and I just want to sit down. I spy Haven and Wyatt in the far corner, he tucks a wayward golden curl behind her ear. They whisper to each other oblivious to anyone else in the room. They are clearly falling in love. I am genuinely happy for them.

I have been broken more than once and glued back together. I need someone who is not afraid of a few leftover cracks, someone who isn't afraid to get cut on a rogue shard. A someone who knows it is not all rainbows and sunshine and good vibes only, that the world can be a terrible place.

I am about four bites in when I hear the commotion. Security has caught a shoplifter. Looks like I will have to fill out an incident report after all.

'The Hole' is packed. My long hair is up in its signature space buns. I am wearing a blue and green striped varsity style shirt complete with a little white collar. My double d's are double d-ing extra hard tonight. My tip jar overfloweth. I have been hit on more times tonight than I have in the last six months. I even got a "that couple over there bought you a drink" proposition, except I am the bartender, so they were just really forward and asked what I was doing after work. If they had offered a few years ago I would have been interested, though my experience with women is limited to when my middle school best friend wanted to "pretend" to make out. You know to be ready for boys. But then she got a new best friend who would pretend without her panties on. C'est la vie.

Haven and Dontae are sitting at the bar tonight, it keeps other less desirable company with the tendency to annoy regulars (Martin exclamation point) from sitting here. I have been laughing my ass off, loudly, and often. I am in an uncharacteristically good mood, almost giddy. It is Saturday, I am off tomorrow, and I know where I will be. And also, who I will be with.

I sit a long neck in front of Haven. I am about to pop the top, I just have to grab the bottle opener I have misplaced on the bar's lower ledge.

"You need help with that?" Another bar patron has sidled up to my friend. A generic dude who starts eyeing her and inevitably her hands.

There is an audible "pop" when I finally get the top off. Haven's deformed hand curls around the glass bottle before she replies, "I'm good."

"Can I help you?" I ask, though he clearly has a buzz already and it is affecting the firing of his neurons.

Ignoring me completely, he watches her take a drink before asking, "Were you born like that?"

"Were you born like that?" She gestures to his body.

"Geez, just trying to make conversation." This idiot obviously cannot read the present company's body language and keeps going, "Do they work like regular hands?"

Oh my God. I am about to tell him to fuck off when Haven replies, "I didn't hear any complaints from your dad last night."

Dontae starts choking on his beer. I chuckle because of course my friend can hold her own.

"Whatever, freak," generic McRude Dude mutters before stumbling off.

"That was annoying," Haven says as another laugh mixes with ours. Fucking Peyton. He is wearing a ball cap with a fishing hook on the brim. His bright blue eyes roam Haven with clear interest. He is low on new prospects these days, but he would be taking her home over my dead body.

"Absolutely not," I say loud and clearly, stating he is barking up the wrong tree.

Peyton flashes his signature panty dropper, his orthodontist must be proud. "Just appreciating the view," he drawls, and Haven blushes. I wonder if I put all of my weight behind the force when I punch him in the face if it would be enough to knock out his front teeth.

Just as I am working out the equation in my head, I notice his sun-kissed boy-next-door good looks are marred by angry red scratches on his arms and neck.

He catches me looking at them with obvious disgust. He smirks, "Take a wild cat to bed you're gonna get scratched."

Ugh. He is so gross. If the world was fair, he would smell like spoilt milk, but of course he does not. The clear clean scent of him is just another one of his wiles to lure innocent women.

He continues to pour the charm on Haven, but she politely declines, unlike me, who declines vehemently.

The phone rings behind me. I hate answering it because it is always a dumb question. Most often, "Are you open?" *Didn't I just answer the phone?*

"The Hole," I yell over the bar's clamor.

"Faye, we've been trying to call your cell." It is my sister, Scarlet. My stomach drops to the sticky floor. My vision tunnels. There is only one reason she is calling. "You need to get over here...it's Dad."

End of life care goes like this, once your loved one tries everything the doctors suggest and the illness is not cured, you get the 'I'm Sorry, There's Nothing More We Can Do' talk, and then you switch to just making them comfortable. Harsh daily medications are traded for pain killers. You get a hospice nurse who comes by daily to check on them (are they dead yet?). You have to buy supplies like a wheelchair and a hospital bed and those toilets that are literally just a bucket in a metal frame. You may eventually have to get IV drip bags, diapers, baby wipes, dry shampoo and possibly some oxygen tanks. Experts can give you a rough estimate of "how long" but six months can stretch to two years. The longer a body holds out, the higher everyone's stress levels tend to get. This is not my dad's first "this is IT"

moment. He has a fever. Maybe he picked up a virus. Maybe maybe maybe. There will not be any testing or hospitalization, we just let it play out.

My mom has retreated to her bedroom. She does not want to be in this room...with him...when IT happens. My sister had to go put my niece back to sleep. I am on the hideous floral love seat listening to my dad breathe, while Kyle lays on the floor using a stuffed animal as a pillow.

"Kyle...thanks for being here for my dad. Thanks for loving him so much," I say into the solemn room.

"He's the only dad I've ever had," he replies.

I kind of knew this, but not the details. Kyle has shit parents, but we have never talked about it. "I told him one time I'd never went fishing. He went out and bought me everything... rod, tackle box...and filled it with all of his favorite lures. Took me out, showed me how to cast. He's a great dad. He's shown me how to be one for the girls."

I am now crying like a little bitch. My sister comes in and sits next me. We manage to put our mutual dislike aside on days like this, just because we do not like each other does not mean we do not love each other. It is complicated and anyways there are bigger feelings to feel at the moment. She does not say anything, just leans her thin body into mine. When she rests her blonde head on me, I wrap my arm around her, and we do what we have been doing. We wait. That is the most fucked up part of this. Is this just a bump in the road or a bad day? Or is this the day we have been waiting for? The day his body finally gives out. The day he actually dies.

CHAPTER 12

Emo, n.:
A Person Who is Overly Sensitive or Emotional

The sky is overcast with ominous clouds ready to spill down at any moment. Black and gray. They match my mood. I rest my chin on my bent knees as I wait. It has been two weeks since I have been here, but it is the usual time. I do not take the path, just parked my car in the same spot before parking myself by the bridge. I have no energy to walk the trail today. My energy has been spent worrying about my dad and then hoping Marcus will come, hoping he will find me.

I am not sure how much time passes before I hear footsteps.

"Hi."

My red rimmed eyes meet his.

"Are you okay?"

I just shake my head.

"Did something happen? I was worried. I tried to look you up on socials, but I didn't even know your last name." He is doing the nervous rambling. His reddish waves are tousled in his artfully unkempt way.

I hate that he may have thought I was not coming back because of something he did or said. "I'm sorry... it's my dad," I answer.

He does not say anything, just watches me with those big open eyes, waiting for me to continue.

"He's really sick. Actually, he's dying."

He winces, "Shit...Faye. That's horrible." He takes a step closer. Stops. Thinks about it and then sits next to me in the grass, our sides flush.

"I feel awful for wishing this...for wishing he would just let go."

Marcus awkwardly puts his arm around me like he has never comforted someone before. "Is this okay?"

"Yeah."

He pats my shoulder stiffly.

"Don't do this often huh?"

"That obvious? I'm more of an introvertabrate," he jokes.

He remains a quiet presence at my side, letting me get the words out.

"Watching my dad waste away slowly day after day is killing me a little bit too. I don't want this version of him to shadow the dad he was..." I start to cry.

Marcus holds me to his side tighter.

"Sorry," I sniffle.

"Stop. Don't apologize." After a moment he says, "I haven't hugged anyone in a while I forgot how warm people are." He says it like it is not the saddest thing I have ever heard, and I cry even harder. I cry for him, and I cry for myself because I have gone weeks and weeks without human touch as well.

He lets me nuzzle into his shoulder while my emotions continue to get the best of me. I better keep an eye out for Aunt Flo, these overactive feelings mean her visit is imminent. Since Marcus always has on baggier clothes, I assumed he was scrawny, but leaning into him he feels anything but.

Bug noise is the only sound until Marcus interrupts it to ask, "Do you know how Scape Ore got its name?"

I shake my head, "No."

"There was a poor woman nearby who had to sell her body to make ends meet. The townsfolk chased her out, torches and pitchforks and whatnot, and she ran here. They did that, instead of asking if she needed help, or, you know, prosecuting the men who took advantage of her. So, this was originally named 'Escaped Whore Swamp,' but I guess to make it more palatable and family friendly, overtime it became Scape Ore. I hope she lived a long life as a swamp witch and cursed those that turned on her."

I smile at his story. I have stopped the waterworks, "Me too."

A commotion sounds on the embankment. A group of what appears to be cryptozoology enthusiasts clamber down it. They are slapping themselves repeatedly in the universal sign of forgotten bug repellent.

"Hey!" one of the group hollers, "You see the Lizardman?"

"Yeah, he went that way." Marcus points towards the footpath.

"Bugs are crazy here," one of the others says.

"Dude it's a swamp," Marcus says, and I turn away to hide my giggle.

The group starts to take pictures and video of their escapade, so we hastily get out of there. Once back at our cars, I turn, "Marcus, let me see your phone."

He hands it over without hesitation and there is no passcode or weird pictures on his lock screen, so I feel completely at ease as I put my number in his contacts. Just as he is about to say something the sky opens, soaking us in seconds. I squeak out a "goodbye!" as I jump in my car feeling like a wet rag inside and out.

Unknown number:
"Did you make it
home okay?"

I get the message and quickly put it into my own contacts before sending him a picture of me in my face mask with R.B. laying on my chest.

F: You?

He sends back a picture of himself wearing a gaming headset. With two finger taps, I heart it, and then I save the picture.

CHAPTER 13

Up, Down, Down, Left, Up, Left, . . . Finish Him

We are meeting for midweek strictly platonic oh-so casual dumplings. It is a nice distraction from my typical weekday tediousness. I am not using the d-word, date—not dick (ok neither of those) because this is not one. But I am going out, so I have to look nice, for me not him. I wear my hair down. It flows down my back like an oil slick to my waist. And I did just get a new skirt in black, my favorite, that I have not had a chance to wear. I tuck my gray v-neck into the fabric where it cinches my middle, enhancing my shape. Let me note here that to achieve an hourglass figure you need ample hips and thighs. Which I do.

Before dinner we are meeting at a comic/games/used-dvd store because both of us love all of the above. Plus, I have not been to this particular shop in ages, but have a vague recollection of it being awesome.

Marcus meets me on the sidewalk dressed straight from work, a gray button-up tucked into black dress pants. The look is done down a bit by a pair of sneakers. I try and fail to notice we are not only matching, but in his closer fitting business casual attire (I was right) he is built much sturdier than I previously thought. Yep, I am doing a great job of not noticing how cute he looks until he smiles at me and the god-damn dimple appears.

"How does your head stay upright with all of that hair?" he muses.

"Ha. Ha. Come on, white-collar boy," I volley back and enter the shop completely ignoring my erratic heartbeat.

"I'm serious, Faye. Does your neck hurt?" he continues to tease, "Can I touch it?"

"Make it fast." I am feigning indifference while flipping through some horror titles when I feel the whisper soft pressure of his fingers. I am sure my cheeks are bright red, but I play it cool. "Get it out of your system?"

"For now," he sighs and stands too close to me as we both look through a graphic novel about zombies.

"Ever wonder why they don't rot?" he asks and I feel his words on my cheek. I am trying not to breathe too deeply because he smells so good, clean and not like bug spray.

"It's the virus…duh." Please let him go to a different section I beg to anyone listening.

"I don't buy it," he mumbles and thankfully meanders off. I relax. Everything is fine. I am fine. Fine.

We spend a ridiculous amount of time in here. Both of us have baskets filled to the brim. I pick up some used video games for the Little Shits, a couple of cult classic films that Marcus has not seen that I do not already own for educational purposes and reading material for me. I just cannot go into a place selling anything with pages and not buy something, or in this case many something's.

There is a nook with a gaming system connected to a tv with a newer fighting game playing in the console. Marcus "ooohhs" before picking up a controller and waggles his eyebrows to me in challenge. The sleeves of his dress shirt are rolled up and it is distracting AF.

I reluctantly pull my eyes away from his forearms and get a closer look at the title. I warn, "I have this at home." He looks skeptical. If there was a moment where I had not planned to annihilate him it is long gone. He is going down. Hard. I should have chosen different words in my own skull, so I shake it clear. Head in the game.

We select our characters. Mine is a sexy humanoid bug girl who not only flies but spews acid spit. He chooses one with a big flashy weapon of course. Silly boys. Alex plays this character all the time, I know his weakness.

"I apologize in advance for kicking your butt," Marcus heckles. "I'll go easy on you at first."

You would think history has shown to never underestimate a woman and if you do, said woman will do everything to prove the naysayer wrong out of spite. (Which is like the world's most powerful motivator.) I do not even reply. Marcus is giddy until it becomes obvious I know what I am doing and I easily win the first round. He looks at me, mouth agape.

"What? I told you I have this game at home, it's not just gathering dust."

"Okay, challenge accepted," he smirks, and widens his stance. He does try harder, but I yawn and again defeat him in round two. We now have a small audience composed of other shoppers. Round three I get to "finish him" with a complicated series of buttons. It is flashy and gory (the Little Shits live for these so of course I had to learn the moves) and I get a few claps of applause.

"That was so hot," someone behind us says.

"Marry me Faye," Marcus begs.

I bat my eyelashes before replying, "Not before dumplings."

It is a short drive to the place Marcus has in mind, so we ride together. When he starts his car, heavy guitar riffs and screaming fills the cab. He blushes and scrambles to turn it down. "Sorry," he mumbles.

"Music, huh? I took you for a podcast guy," I tease.

He shakes his head, "Not really, no. I guess you're a podcast gal?"

My face must light up because he smiles when I answer, "Most definitely."

His eyes have left me to pay attention to the road, "What about?"

"Anything morbid, macabre and murderous." I waggle my brows which were freshly waxed yesterday.

"Sorry to disappoint you, Faye, but I don't do the murdery stuff. I'm more interested in what humans do with their brains and hands to create...not destroy."

I feel a snick in my chest cavity. A dead bolt slides back. Then a chain jangles as I unlatch it. Followed by:

Click.

Click.

Click.

Click.

As each lock is turned, the heavy iron door opens to reveal the very thing that now stretches and unfurls after its long slumber. My heart.

I slip into a booth and jump when Marcus follows behind me. "So we can read together," he explains with a shrug. His arm grazes mine and I shiver.

Dumplings are ordered. We sip hot green tea from little ornate china cups and share a comic he just bought. The quiet between us would not be awkward if I were not having my internal freak out. He is younger than me, he is not as hefty as me, he is etc. etc. The restaurant is quaint and obviously a spot frequented by locals. I desperately grasp for something to talk about, so I ask, "How do you know about this place?"

"I grew up here," he says, not looking up from his page. His hair would fall into his eyes if not for his glasses.

"In this dumpling shop," I mess with him.

"Almost, but not quite I'm afraid...just fifteen minutes down the road." Our food has arrived and he expertly wields his chopsticks to stuff a dumpling in his mouth ending further elaboration.

"You gonna visit the 'rents afterwards or something?" I pry.

He is not put off by my questioning and politely finishes chewing before answering. "Nah. I try to keep visits scarce. I uh...don't really have a close relationship with them. Not like you. Put it this way I wouldn't check in on my dad everyday."

"That sucks. If it's any consolation, it's just my dad...if my home was a hurricane, my dad is the eye of the storm. Make sense? Sadly, not uncommon, my mom has always been my first and most formidable bully." I sigh through my nose.

"You're right, not uncommon, mine cares so much what everyone thinks and terrorizes me because of it. My mom has always obsessed over my skin. Once she realized it would never be perfect, she started getting our family pictures edited. Don't get me wrong they did the required shelter, feed and clothe thing. They're just preoccupied with golf games and luncheons at the country club." He shrugs. Our arms graze again.

"Is that why you live with your grandfather?" I continue with the questions.

"I haven't lived with my parents since I graduated, but found myself needing to relocate. I was in a pinch, and he offered his second bedroom. Also, my granddad can use help, but is too stubborn to ask. He doesn't get around like he used to, so I cut the grass and make sure he gets to his checkups. As a bonus I've set him up with satellite internet and a giant tv so he can watch the Discovery Channel in high def."

"*Swamp People* I hope." We have polished off dinner and are now on the dregs of the tea pot.

He shakes his head. "He loves that guy that always has his arm in a cow."

I chuckle. "Yeah, that's a good one. Quality programming."

He parks next to my car and before he can say anything or I have time to overthink, I lean over to kiss the rough skin of his cheek. I then exit with a "Goodnight, Marcus" before I do something rash like climb into his lap or even more ludicrous like keep him forever. I have repeatedly reminded myself all evening that this is not a good time for me. This is actually the worst possible time. I am a mess, however, a hot one.

"Text me when you get home," he says, then waits until I get in, buckle up and start my car, before driving away.

I see his text bubble, full of dots, appear and disappear and then reappear again.

I want to scream.

My finger hovers over the black heart emoji. Don't you dare send that Faye. Don't you do it.

I enter the big top with excitement. While mid beauty routine last night, I missed the arrival of the newest addition to our show. The circus has tigers and elephants and trapeze artists flying high above the house, but the freaks, we are the real stars. Being the Bearded Lady, I am one that shines the brightest. String lights twinkle like fireflies in the shadows of the red and white striped tent. I wear my cornflower blue dress for this first impression. It brings out my eyes.

There. Standing next to our Ring Master, discussing his act. The top button of his shirt is open showing just a sliver of his chest. Strong hands are on his slim hips. His head full of auburn hair, nods along. Even with skin covered in scales he is handsome. This man is bound to draw a crowd. His head slowly lifts, and our eyes meet. The skin around his face crinkles with lines as he smiles, showing teeth straight and white. A dimple indents his left cheek. I suck in air as my stomach drops all the way to my satin slipper clad toes. The Roustabouts finish hanging the newcomer's banner, the canvas unfurls behind him with a flutter. The block letters hand painted just yesterday in anticipation of another performer. Well hello, Lizardman. Hello, indeed.

It is still dark when I wake. I guess business casual is what my dreams are made of. I lay awake and try not to think about dimples or the way his hand felt on my hair until my alarm goes off.

Filler, n.:
A Thing put in a Space to Fill it

I am rolling through my nightly skin routine when my phone pings. It is 2 am.

M: Did you make it home from the bar ok

F: Marcus why are you awake…its the witching hour

M: I just finished a 6 hour quest in WOW

F: You are the biggest dork I have ever met

M: Does this mean you won't go to a renfest with me

F: No way I love a smoked turkey leg

M: Huzzah!

F: Never mind

Beep. Beep. Beep. Beep. Beep. Beep. Beep. Beep. Beep.

The sound of the scanner has imprinted itself on my brain so deeply nothing can drown out its echoes. I worry I will still hear it when I am six feet under rotting away.

My feet and back ache from standing eight hours minus two fifteen and one thirty-minute break. At least only half a dozen customers complained about inflation and only one old man told me I would be prettier if I smiled.

Miss Ruby's much crisper missing poster is tacked next to Mandy's faded one. Their photocopied eyes stare out to nothing. Nothing at all.

Today is bath day for my dad. Kyle and I wash his emaciated body down with sponges while he repeatedly apologizes to us for needing help to bathe. Afterward, I will trim his toenails.

In my car I start to fill with dread. It rises, bubbling up from somewhere deep like geothermal activity under the earth's crust. I am about to erupt. I do not know how much longer

I can do this. Something is lodged in my throat. I cannot breathe. I need to scream or puke or both. I feel sweaty.

My phone vibrates just loud enough to hear over my panic. A message from Marcus. It is a picture of a Halloween store set up in what looks like what was once a bank.

M: Code Orange!!

A huff of air leaves my nostrils in a sad excuse for a laugh, but it is just enough to clear my airways. To calm the rising tide. I sit there breathing.

In.

Out.

I will not choke. I will not give up today. I will keep going. Doing what I have to do.

CHAPTER 14

Babysitter's Club

I shared my location and ultimately my address. Marcus reciprocated and now I watch with anticipation as his little dot gets closer and closer on the phone app. My living space is never gross-gross, with it just being me and one cat, but I may have put a little extra elbow grease into my regularly scheduled day off cleaning. I even lit a candle that is currently wafting apple-cinnamon-scented plumes into the air.

Anxious, I jump at the sound of crunching gravel through the open window. Then I leave Alex and Oscar, too engrossed in their game to pay me any mind. By the time he is out of his car and at the stairs leading up to my apartment, I have met him on the bottom step. He is back in a gamer shirt and (I pause a moment to close my eyes and raise my face to the sky for composure) gray sweatpants.

"I started to panic on the way here because I didn't bring anything...was I supposed to bring something?" I start to answer but he keeps going. "It's rude to show up empty handed, isn't it? I'm such a jerk." He continues to voice his etiquette crisis while I navigate my own personal one happening inside my head. He runs his hands through his hair ruffling it further.

"It's fine. Stop it."

He had been avoiding making too much eye contact but takes a good look at me then. I already know what he is thinking.

I am in baggy top and biker shorts, my hair is knotted into a messy bun atop my head, and I am not wearing any makeup. "I'm letting my face breathe."

His eyes roam over me once more. I am becoming a tad self conscious when he says, "You're so beautiful. Are you real or am I dreaming?"

That was not what I was expecting. "As real as you," I reply. No foundation or concealer plus his words equal very red cheeks.

"I must be dreaming. Why would you spend time with someone like me?" His green eyes look to mine in earnest.

"Don't talk about my friend like that," I cut him off.

"Is that what we are...friends?" I swear his voice has gone an octave deeper.

"I think we are at the part where we're figuring it out." I start up the stairs before I say anything else.

Marcus follows me quietly contemplating until about halfway up. "Uhhh...what is all this?" He points to the bird carcasses left on the stairs. Feathers and bone bits are strewn across the landing.

"Abandon all hope, ye who fly here," I reply cheekily. "R.B.'s victims. His little trophies. If I leave them here until they're dried crispy husks, he is content to play with the remains and doesn't murder more defenseless birds."

"You enable his psychotic tendencies," his tone playful.

"That is literally the definition of love," I reply.

Marcus snickers from behind me.

"I should've seen it coming with all of the bed wetting and fire starting." He pushes me inside.

Once we are through the door, he takes his time, slowly absorbing all he sees. He leaves his shoes by the door along side the boy's smaller ones, on my coffin shaped welcome mat that is printed with the word "goodbye." After an exaggerated inhalation he says, "It smells really good in here."

Oscar replies from the couch, only the top of his dark head visible, "Faye's making nachos."

"And cookies," I add, getting the attention of all three of them.

Alex does a double take when he notices I am not alone. "Who the hell are you?" His brows make a straight line as he bunches his forehead.

"Marcus, meet the Little Shits next door, Alex and Oscar. Little Shits, this is Marcus." I do some finger waggling between them as Marcus makes his way over to sit on the couch as far away from them as possible. A moment later Marcus jumps, thanks to the orange cat that has materialized out of thin air.

"I've never come face to face with a serial killer." He stares into the depths of R.B.'s luminescent orbs.

"You are being weighed and measured, my friend," I reply from the kitchen where I put the finishing touches on our lunch.

"Just give Rat Bastard bites of your food and he'll like you," Oscar offers.

"Aaahh, should you be saying words like that?" Marcus is apparently scandalized by my lackadaisical babysitting.

"Dude, calm down. They're older models and come with that feature," I reply in defense while joining the group and lay the tray of nachos before them.

The boys back me up. "Yeah we're twelve and thirteen. We're just small for our age, but Faye told us size doesn't matter," Oscar says cheerfully. Always my hero. Alex is still glaring at

Marcus who is currently choking on a cheese laden tortilla chip. I slap his back.

"Are you Faye's boyfriend?" Alex interrogates.

"I am a man thank you…and yes we are friends." He looks to me pointedly and I roll my eyes.

"Do you kiss and stuff?" Oscar asks innocently while Marcus turns beet red.

"And stuff? Really?" I rebuke.

"We're in middle school we know things," Oscar shrugs.

"None of your business. Gentlemen do not kiss and tell… you got it?" They both nod in acceptance and stuff their faces.

"Wait. Do you have a different girlfriend?" Alex is not done with the third degree.

"I do not," Marcus answers.

I am relieved at this news.

"Good, because Faye doesn't play second fiddle." Oscar's reply makes Marcus look to me questioningly.

"We had an issue with two timing last year with a girl in his gym class." I wave my hand to brush off further details.

"Have you ever had one?" Alex asks.

I am so glad they have no filters and are doing the heavy lifting for me.

I smile at his obvious discomfort. Marcus squirms a little before answering, "A few, yes."

"Any serious?" I add.

He cuts me a sharp glance, "I lived with someone up until a year ago." So that is why he needed to 'relocate.'

"Did she break your heart?" Oscar asks sadly. He is so damn cute.

"Not exactly," Marcus mumbles. "We just drifted apart...and she really wanted kids. And no offense guys...I don't."

I did not think my heart could swell anymore, but damn if it doesn't.

"Faye doesn't want kids either," Oscar says.

"Stop telling all my secrets. Are we playing video games or what?" I interrupt.

Thankfully show and tell is over.

There is a light knock at the front door followed by a chorus of "Mom's here" from the boys. I wave her in without taking my hands off my controller somehow. The four of us are on a mission. R.B. is draped over Oscar's shoulders like a fox stole. Their mom makes small talk.

"Tina, Marcus, Marcus, Tina," I introduce them without taking my eyes off the screen. "My dudes it is time to wrap this up."

The boys groan, causing Marcus to chuckle.

Alex and Oscar jump around telling her about all the games we can now play with an even number of players. I wink at Marcus. "They've revealed my true motive for bringing you here."

As they leave, they take all the noise with them. The quiet between us is almost deafening. We are alone.

We share a look before Marcus jumps up to clean the dishes. "I guess I'll wash these, then go," he trails off.

I follow him the few steps into my little kitchen, "You can stay."

"Okay."

I laugh at his hasty response. "What if I said stay for a murder marathon."

"I'll cover my eyes during the gory parts." He places the now clean dishes on their drying rack.

I lean on the island. "Fine we'll watch one of the movies I just bought."

"The bird one?" I am trying not to notice him ogling where my shirt dips while also being slightly horrified he is calling the cult classic and one of my favorite films this.

"I can not believe you just said that," I mumble. "But yes, the 'bird' one." I add finger quotations.

While I set up the entertainment, Marcus inspects my bookshelves, reading spines and fingering the tchotchkes in between. He pulls out a title, "Romance, huh?"

"Keep reading..." I tease.

His eyes widen, "What would you do with two of those?"

I giggle like a god-damn schoolgirl. "I'd be clutching my pearls if I was wearing some."

He shakes his head. He picks up the framed picture of Mandy and me, dressed as Romy and Michelle, one Halloween. We are both laughing, scantily clad and covered in post it notes.

"I couldn't sit down in that dress," I admit and smile sadly at the memory of that night.

Done with his perusal we align ourselves on my couch—at a respectable distance, I might add—and settle in for the movie. My shorts have ridden up and Marcus points to my thigh where an inked vine peeks out. "Will you show me this?" he asks, and I think of the laundry list of what else I could "show him."

I roll the clingy fabric up revealing the large pumpkin tattooed there. "My dad calls me Pumpkin, and you know being a white girl it's in our DNA to love them."

"What's not to love about pumpkins?" He says as I roll my shorts back down. We make direct eye contact and I will my pupils into a heart shape. I try to psychically transmit the words "kiss me" into his brain—long over any fears about us. Fuck caution to the wind as they say. I do that thing you read about in books where the girl bites her lip to draw attention to her mouth. I think it works when his eyes dip down, but he just swallows and then turns his attention back to the movie. I suppress my sigh and inevitable disappointment and sink further into the couch. Maybe it will swallow me. Luckily, I do not spend too much time over analyzing everything because I drift off to sleep.

"Faye." A light touch on my face wakes me. I am too comfortable to be embarrassed I am using Marcus as a body pillow. "I'm going to go," he says softly, his voice just above my head.

I nestle further into his chest, "Just stay."

He nods, and I fall...

CHAPTER 15

Cuddling produces Oxytocin which Promotes a sense of Calmness, Relaxation and even Happiness

I love this time of night. The Barkers are out front calling to the Rubes. "Step right up folks! See it with your own eyes!" Hidden fans blow the scents of cooking confections to further their interest. We will have a full house.

I am just adding finishing touches to my hair when there is a light rapping at the opening of my tent. Hmmmm. There is a support pole out there I guess one could knock. I satisfy my curiosity and walk toward the sound.

Oh. My caller has me speechless. "Hi." The Lizardman is awkwardly lingering there. He puts his hands in his pockets looking like he is about to kick rocks.

"I usually use a colored light, but it was suggested maybe you'd have a better idea to make me look a little green?"

I am known to have a good eye for these things and a plethora of cosmetics to achieve it. I beckon him to follow me inside.

We have spoken only a handful of words. Mostly we share longing looks. I catch him staring at me and brazenly hold his gaze. I sit him down at my vanity. It is a gaudy thing. I have been chastised by the set hands about its unpractical weight, but I do not care. I make the circus a lot of money and I am spoiled because of it. Besides, they do not cry about the enormous size of the Fat Lady's bed. He is silent, except for his soft even breathing as he patiently waits for me to find the jar I am looking for, an emerald luster powder. Subtle. Yet the shine will be dazzling under the house lights. "This may tickle," I warn him. My voice gone raspy. I ignore my fluttering heartbeat as I swoop the brush over his cheeks. I cannot look anywhere but the textured skin where I work. His eyes bore into me. This close I notice his green irises have flecks of gold in them. I see his throat bob when he swallows. As I lean over, my apricot colored dress dips, giving peeks of the creamy skin the fabric covers. The temperature spikes. I feel flush.

"Close your eyes." He does as he's told. I blow an errant hair from his cheek before thinking better of it. "An eyelash," I rush to explain. Our faces so close. Practically touching.

"You're so beautiful. Are you even real?" he whispers into me.

"As real as you." One of us just has to close the distance. I know once we start this, we will not be able to stop. Just a slight shift and then our lips *barely touch when a loud crash interrupts us. Both of our heads whip toward the sound, then go to investigate. Outside, the Fat Lady sits on the splinters of yet another broken chair. A crowd of spectators has gathered to watch the Strongman wrap his ginormous arms around her waist and pull her to her feet. I look to the man beside me, now shimmering with a green sheen and even more attractive. He bends down to whisper into my ear, his lips grazing my lobe, "To be continued." I watch as he walks into the crowd.*

A shrill noise cuts through the dream. I become aware of the chest under my cheek, the heart enclosed by it beats steady, if not a little fast. "Yeah, Hi. Sorry, I stayed at my friend's house. I'm okay, thanks for calling." I move a little to watch Marcus as he sets his phone back on the coffee table and gets his glasses. "Sorry to wake you, my granddad noticed I didn't come home last night." I am still draped over him, so I feel his words as they rumble through his body. He must have covered us sometime in the night with the blanket that hung on the back of my couch.

"We had a sleepover," I murmur, still half asleep. Maybe if I were not, I would be mortified that I had practically drooled on him. I stretch a little and yawn. It makes him yawn too. "You yawned. That means you're not a psychopath."

"Oh good, I took an online questionnaire one time that had me worried," he responds sarcastically. The arm he has around my back squeezes. "You're wrong you know."

I widen my eyes, "What...you're a psychopath?"

He tickles my side. "No, you fiend. We've already figured it out."

I snuggle further into his side and say into him, "Oh yeah, what's that?"

"I've never liked anyone as much as I like you," he says into my hair. "You're like my best friend and more."

I lift a little to look at him. "Then why haven't you kissed me?" My dream is still vividly playing on loop in my head.

"I'm shy. Why haven't you kissed me?" His lips turn up to a coy smile.

"I can't reach." He obliges and pulls me higher onto him.

"I'll squish you."

He ignores my words and touches his lips to mine. I am still a little sleepy and overly sensitive as he moves his fingers over the exposed skin of my leg, which is entwined with his. He starts to kiss down my neck when the alarm on my phone screams reminding me I have work today.

"Shit." I am panting. A little.

He whispers into my ear, "To be continued..." making me shudder at my dreams coming true. I have a vague thought...I hope not all of them.

CHAPTER 16

The Average Person will spend One-Third of their Life at Work -Roughly 90,000 Hours-

Unsurprisingly my schedule does not allow for much free time. I meet Marcus at a halfway point for lunch between my jobs. I was a little worried there would be an awkwardness between us, but as soon as he sees me his face breaks into a wide smile. I do not even hesitate to throw myself at him and maul him. He encourages me with his matching enthusiasm, as we eat each other's faces. He pulls my hair out of its tie and delves his hand in the waves.

Later that evening as I cross the parking lot of the bar, a dragonfly lands on my arm. I am already in a great mood. Now I am in awe. Nature is so beautiful. I turn my limb this way and that to admire the purples and turquoises that gleam on the creature's wings when it fucking bites me. I did not even know they bite. I shake it off, completely miffed.

Our next rendezvous was supposed to be dinner, but we ended up spending the time in the back of my car. Marcus stops teasing me about my "toaster" when he realizes how much space there is—when the seats fold down—to ravish each other. His glasses fog up just like the car's windows. I am equal parts surprised and delighted when his hand slipped under my waistband after asking permission. I return the favor and got to finally hear him say the f-word, while his face is buried in my neck.

When we are apart Marcus texts me what sounds akin to open mic poetry. "The color blue makes me miss you." "I can't sleep...I smell you on my skin." I am like a teenaged girl with her first two-hundred-year-old vampire, and I might be falling irrevocably in love with him.

Soft snores are the only noise in the otherwise empty house. I am sitting with my dad while the rest of the family partakes in some preschool hubbub for my niece. I am simultaneously playing a game with Marcus, while also texting him innuendos. I smile smugly at his reply.

"What's got you smiling like that?" I look over to the hospital bed where my dad watches me, finally awake. He sleeps most of the time now.

"A friend of mine," I answer. "You need anything?"

He groans as he tries to adjust himself in the bed. "Sit me up a bit?"

I get off my ass to help him rearrange his pillows and then hand him a drink from the fridge. I even put a little bendy straw in it.

After a few sips he asks, "Is this a friend or a friieeennnd?" He smirks over the aluminum can at my warming cheeks.

"Both." Yeah that sounds about right.

Dad closes his eyes. "Good. I'm so happy you have someone. I worry you're lonely...and that you're not happy."

"I don't need someone else to be happy, Dad. I'm fine being alone," I defend myself and fellow single cat ladies everywhere.

He chuckles lightly. "I know, Pumpkin. It just makes me feel better. Times have been tough for you and I know I'm not helping," he adds.

"Don't...say things like that." He is making me emotional.

"Okay fine. I'll drop it. Do you have a picture?"

I just finished my lunch with Dontae. Sometimes we get lucky, and our break times overlap. He spent the time showing me apartment options and I promised I would go with him to see the spaces in person sometime in the upcoming weeks. We have skipped the monthly meet up twice now, all of us preoccupied with other things or people: Haven and I savoring our new relationships, Dontae finalizing his move and the twins...well they only need each other it seems. I have an emergency root touch-up scheduled right after my shift. My nail fill was done yesterday. I am back to black. I am thinking I should add a bikini wax to my scheduled beauty maintenance, you know, just in case.

To avoid a crowd of soccer moms congregating in the main aisle, I make a left down the one with box after box of cereal and almost run into Martin. I glance behind me to see if I can backtrack without notice when I hear him say, "Please talk to me, Faye."

I check the time on my phone. "You've got six minutes before I have to clock back in."

He nods. Martin still has much of his defensive line physique. Though his shirt stretches across his broad shoulders, he has a bit of a dad-bod these days. As far as I know he is not a dad, nor have I seen him date anyone for years.

He chokes on the words before finding his voice, "She wanted me to tell you..." he starts. "I had it all planned. I was going to apologize for the bullying and then beg for your forgiveness. Because I am in love with your best friend."

I swallow down the bile filling my mouth. I am hot and cold at the same time. Tears stream from his tawny eyes. Begrudgingly, I am moved by the sight of them. "I asked her to marry me on our second date," he sniffles. "From the moment I met her, I knew Mandy was the one."

"How long?" I croak out.

"About a year…not long enough…before…" He trails off not wanting to finish that thought. The signs were there. Mandy had stopped seeing her sneaky links because she was ready for something real. It seems she found it, and she did not think she could tell me because I am a shitty friend.

Still crying, he continues, "She told me she had her baby names all picked out…Lucy for a girl and for a boy…"

"Louie," we say in unison. Oh, how wrong I have been. Hating this man when we could have been shoulders for each other to lean on. Fuck. Fuck. Fuck.

"I'm so sorry," I say.

It is all so unfair. Mandy should be here with us, with him, and their future babies with matching L names. When someone leaves us, we mourn not only them and the futures they never had, but the experiences we can not share with them. We keep losing again and again.

"I gotta get to work." Like a coward I leave him standing there. I have had enough for one day.

"I can come to 'The Hole,' Marcus' voice rings out from the speaker in my car as I drive.

"And do what?" I ask incredulously.

"Sit at the bar." At his answer I burst out in laughter just picturing him on a stool sandwiched between some regulars.

"Do you even drink?" I spit out.

"No...it causes my skin to flare up...Do you?" he volleys back.

"Working as a bartender makes drinking alcohol lose its luster pretty fast...but no you can't come sit at the bar, you'll distract me. And I don't want to subject you to the debauchery that happens there." He starts a rebuttal when I cut him off rudely. "Anyways, it doesn't matter because I'm putting in my two weeks today."

Technically, I do not have to work this much. I originally picked up the second job to save for travel and/or possible relocation. I never ended up making any concrete plans because whenever I thought about making some, I would put it off and six months would go by. Now I work so much because I just do not have anything else to do. Working more hours than not I have been able to keep my mind off all the things I do not want to think too deeply about. "After my dad passes..." my voice stronger than I thought it would be, "I want to travel. I'd like to see some mountains."

"Like camping?" he asks, too perky in my opinion.

"Ew, Marcus, no..." I shudder at the thought of sleeping in a tent.

"Can I go?" I can picture his full bottom lip in a pout as he asks.

"Obviously…you're driving. So I can look at the outside safely from my passenger window."

The hickey covered bus boy is in his usual spot scrubbing pots. "I hope you're using protection," I say to him as I pass, inhaling the musty scent of restaurant kitchen. I may miss it a smidge.

Miss Irene is in her chair peeling potatoes. Miss Innes is at the stove stirring today's special, shrimp and grits, in shoes without holes in them. Cook is shoveling food into his tattoo covered face. I watch them share this space, their meal, and a laugh. They notice me at once and yell, "Faye's here!" I am handed a ramekin of food and brought into the fold. Isn't it funny how you really do become a little like family when you spend so much time together with people who are happy to see you for no other reason than you showed up? Trevor comes in greeting me with a proud smile as he presents his graded college assignments to show me how well he did. My eyes swell with tears, but I will them back into their ducts because I have been doing way too much crying lately and my eyeliner is perfect today. Time to ruin everyone's good mood. Time to quit my job.

CHAPTER 17

Make Damn Sure

There is a buzzing in the air tonight. It could be the crowd's excitement, or the strain the shoddy extension cords and over-used outlets put on the local power grid. Maybe it is the surge of adrenaline that comes from riding each steel death trap. Or the culinary options that all induce high blood pressure and instant diabetes. Or maybe it is just the feeling that comes once a year from standing in a field that has been cultivated, crops harvested and now holds something different. Something feral. A carnival.

The sky is putting on a show above the festivities. The pink-purple dusk, a perfect backdrop to the lights that blink everywhere our eyes can see. Marcus and I have brought the Little Shits to this money pit without one ounce of hesitation. Their joy is infectious.

Our foursome inches down the midway. Savory and sweet scents perfume the air—butter drenched popcorn, sickly sweet cotton candy, foot long corn dogs, tooth chipping sugar lacquered apples and more for the taking. We settle on ribbon thin potatoes smothered in nacho cheese and deep-fried battered sandwich cookies, whose hydrogenated oils have altered to a cocoa flavored goo. I hand the boys napkins to wipe clean the powdered sugar mustaches on their upper lips. Their pupils are dilated with artificial sweeteners and anticipation.

My attention is everywhere: lights, sounds and carnie ghouls, but I find Marcus' eyes on me. "What?" I ask sharply. "Do I have cheese on my face?" I am going to pay for these goodies with gastrointestinal distress later, but they are worth it.

He watches my hand run over my mouth to wipe away any offensive unnatural orange goodness with intensity. "Stop. Your face is perfect." He bats my hand away, smiling as my cheeks heat.

"Okay, so what's the plan?" I ask Alex and Oscar.

"We want to ride that!" Alex points to something that will surely make me vomit after our deep-fried treats. Their height just barely makes it to the you-must-be-this-tall-to-ride line.

"Yeah, that's a no for me." The wind picks up the ends of my hair. I am second guessing wearing it down even though Marcus can not take his eyes off the dark strands. I am delighted with how much he loves my hair.

"That's a no for me as well," Marcus agrees. Fall is heavy in the air. He wears a black beanie and coordinating flannel. With the worst of his dermatological abnormalities covered, he looks like just another attendee.

"Why did you get those then?" Alex points to the "all you can ride" band Marcus is currently fiddling with, the only indicator he is nervous in the bustling crowd.

"To ride that." I point a long onyx nail at the Ferris wheel. "And that." I point at the funhouse.

"Borrrriiiinnnggg," the boys sing song.

"Okay then, you go shake up your entrails and we will do the boring rides. Let's plan to meet back in this spot in two hours to check in with each other. Stay together."

The brothers shout their agreement at me as they take off running to stand in line at a thrill ride.

Marcus takes my hand. I weave my fingers through his. Warmth spreads all the way up my arm as I lead him to the funhouse entrance. The façade is the gaping mouth of a devil.

Once through the red face, paint peeling from its nationwide tour, we creep through a low-lit corridor where hidden jets burst frigid air onto us. Hands still linked, we run across a rickety bridge to a hall of mirrors. Our reflections stretch and shrink, I snap a picture of our distended shapes.

Next, we are in a tight hallway, completely dark except for an exit sign a few feet away. Marcus pulls me to a stop. "Wait a second," he whispers behind me.

"You okay?" I feel around for him. My hand finds his chest, it lifts in time to his heartbeat as it pounds through the cotton of his shirt. "Are you scared?" I tease.

"Terrified," he replies. Fingers find my face just before his lips do. When he deepens the kiss, I smash my body into his. It is a miracle my weight does not knock him over.

Laughter from other oncoming patrons break our spell. I graze his bottom lip with my teeth before pulling him towards the exit. I hear him make a noise as I climb the ladder at the end. I am glad I wore these jeans.

I slide down the metal chute, landing hard on my ass, thankful for the extra fluff cushioning my bones there. I roll out of the way just before Marcus hits and yank him over to me. With an unspoken agreement we begin making out on the grass.

"Bruh, this a family establishment." The two of us are chastised by a carnie with a cigarette hanging out of his mouth equal parts tobacco and discarded ash.

"Sorry," Marcus apologizes and grabs my outstretched hand to haul me up. "Faye, we have been reprimanded by a guy wearing a 't and a all day' shirt."

"It means 'turtles and alligators' you perverts!" he yells at our backs as we run to the Ferris wheel in a hysterical fit of laughter.

The lap bar barely finishes lowering before we are on each other again, vaguely aware of the seat rocking. Creaking sounds as the metal box we are in continues to teeter. I am all at once keenly aware of the intensity of the affection I am plying Marcus with and, thanks to my voluptuous thighs, the bar keeping us in is practically useless. For our safety I ease off a little. Night has fully settled in; the stars are washed out by the carnival's electric light. His arm weaves around my back, I rest my head on his shoulder, and everything is so damn perfect.

It is late as the four of us drive back to my apartment. The boys are subdued, it is way past their bedtime. A song plays softly from the speaker. "I love this song." I turn it up when I recognize the chords as an Emo ballad of my youth. I start to sing along at a modest level, practically whispering the lyrics, until Marcus joins me at the chorus. We scream at the top of our lungs in unison. We are off key and incredibly ridiculous, but this is like one of those scenes from a movie where everything is so perfect—it is like it was written just for us. I am laughing so hard. His eyelashes are wet spikes from his tears of mirth, and I know if anyone were watching us on screen right now, they would be thinking these characters are in love.

Alex's voice rings loud and clear from the backseat reminding me we do in fact have an audience, "That song was mid at best!" We bust out laughing again.

We say our goodbyes to the boys. Marcus walks me to my door, "I guess I better go..." his words trail off as I pull him inside. Our shoes slip off our feet, I tug the beanie from his head, and with linked hands lead him to my bedroom.

CHAPTER 18

On Average it takes Men 97 days to Express their Feelings of Love, while for Women it takes around 139 days

I will not sit still. I am so nervous. I pace inside the tent until there, the soft sound of approaching footsteps. The Lizardman shyly pulls back the canvas just enough to enter my tent. Golden candlelight illuminates the curves of my body, dressed only in a night shift.

Never taking his eyes from mine, he opens his hand, in it the scrap of paper I slipped into his palm, facing up. I can read the words in their flowing script, "Come to me tonight." He lets it fall. His lips on mine before the paper reaches the ground. His hands are everywhere, greedy to feel everything hidden under the flimsy silk. I am on fire. He trails kisses down my neck. I gasp. I pull down the straps of his suspenders one at a time. Then move to the buttons of his shirt as he licks and bites my throat. I push the shirt from his shoulders as he lifts me. My legs wrap around his waist. His tongue is in my mouth, deep dancing with my own. Twirling incessantly. Going deeper and deeper. I feel the fork at the end licking my mouth.

I gag. I try to pull back. My mouth is filling with water. I choke. Unable to catch a breath, my lungs ache as I push him away. He lowers me. Hurt and confusion written on his face as I run out. As soon as my feet touch blades of grass I collapse and retch. Water spews from me. Leaves, sticks and grasses nick my gullet like razor blades, broken glass. And water, so much black murky water leaves my body in wave after dirty wave.

I can finally suck in cool night air. So much I cough. My body heaves until I grab what is stuck in my throat. With fingers shoved in there, until reaching the end of the obstruction. I pull.

It is long strands of yellow hair.

My body jerks. Marcus stirs behind me. He rolls closer and then asks "You okay?" into my bare shoulder.

I touch my phone screen, 3:33 am. "Yeah just a bad dream."

He snuggles my body from behind, his arm coming around my waist. "You're okay. I've got you." Instead of his words comforting me I lay awake and stare into the dark room, my throat raw and aching.

A blood curdling scream wrenches me out of my thoughts and back to reality. I should have called out sick, but we had our monthly mandatory meeting, not to be confused with the seasonal mandatory meeting or the biannual corporate policy meeting. I walked in on two hours of sleep chanting the word "benefits" to "woo-sah" me through this fuckery. A disheveled mother and her red-faced banshee have entered my line. I can barely concentrate on checking out her order, my mind out of sorts. This has less to do with my lack of sleep and everything to do with the man who kept me awake. I finish the transaction before letting myself slip into last nights reruns.

Being my size, it is a little daunting exposing all of myself. Yes, there are voluptuous curves, but also rolls of creamy skin. Beautiful, smooth, and soft creamy skin but a lot of it. I know I would have been a target if there was really a man keeping larger ladies in a hole in his basement to make a human flesh suit. I put the lotion on the skin. (Though I am too much of a cynical asshole to help someone put a couch, let alone anything in a van. Manufacturers, please stop making windowless vans.)

When Marcus squeezes the space where my hip rounds out, the lace of my panties stretches tight, I almost feel self conscious until he admits, "I love this." Then his hands move higher. "I love these," he says reverently and buries his face in the place his hands just left. And then, "I love you." The words spoken directly into my mouth so I can feel them on my tongue. I swallow them. Those three words. They fill me in a way no other words ever have before. Because I know I feel exactly the same. And when his rough skin moves against mine, I do not mind at all.

Our perfect night, I am sure is the first of many. Maybe every night from now on will be perfect. I should be positively buoyant, aglow with post-coital bliss. I should be transforming the dot on every "i" I write into a little heart. But my dream last night, it lingers, like the ghost of my friend who will forever haunt me. I know her body is most likely decaying somewhere, at this point there probably is not much left. A few scattered bones tangled in her long blonde hair.

I barely make it to the bathroom before I lose my shoddy breakfast, just a granola bar, since my stomach has been upset. I am only a little surprised to see murky black liquid did not gush from my body. At the sink, I splash cool clean water on my face. My eyeliner runs down my pale cheeks.

Tillie exits a nearby stall. "You coming down with something?" she asks, concerned, while she washes her hands the dozens of bracelets on her wrists jingle, grabbing my attention from my reflection. I look deranged. Oh, I am coming down with something all right...a big fat case of guilt.

After work, I add insult to injury and visit my dad. By this hour of the day the bags under my eyes have their own bags. He shoos me off, somehow still able to worry about me from his deathbed. Which ultimately makes me feel worse.

Outside my door, Marcus waits for me in one of the wicker chairs, R.B. in his lap getting lathered with attention. By his feet is a bag of groceries in a reusable bag (of fucking course). He had texted me earlier saying he wanted to cook me dinner and we can play house. He just made me more upset because he is so cute and wonderful, and I am not sure I even deserve him.

"Hey," I greet, my misery written all over my face.

"Everything okay?" he asks with trepidation.

"How can I be happy, Marcus? What's wrong with me?"

He pushes R.B. off his lap and pulls me into the spot the cat vacated.

He runs his hand in soothing strokes down my back, not saying anything while he chooses his words carefully. "You're not forgetting what happened to Mandy...or what's happening with your dad...but wouldn't they want you to be happy? If it was you...wouldn't you want that for them?"

"I haven't even been back to the swamp. I just stopped going. I haven't done anything. And I feel like I failed some kind of test."

He stays quiet, just continues to pet me like he did R.B., offering me comfort. "Have you considered...that maybe the Universe wasn't sending you to Scape Ore to look for clues? Maybe your spirit guides brought you there so we could meet. I mean we probably wouldn't have otherwise. Maybe they wanted you to have something good."

I look up at him. His auburn hair wet on the ends from the quick shower he must have had. His green eyes look into mine from behind his glasses with sincerity.

"Yeah..." is all I can reply as I cup his cheek, still unsure if I deserve anything decent.

"We can take the trail this weekend." He pauses, and I can see there is something else he wants to say. "Um...would you want to meet my granddad while we're there? You don't have to if you don't want to, I just figured..."

I kiss him to keep him from rambling. His favorite anxious pastime. "That would be wonderful."

I do not get to say anything else because things get hot and heavy. So heavy the wicker chair starts to break. We finally go inside so I can see what Marcus has in mind when we play house. It certainly improves my mood.

CHAPTER 19

It was Seven Foot Tall, had Red Glowing Eyes and it was Covered in Scales

Marcus' granddaddy sits on the front porch of his small house in a classic rocking chair. Comically, he wears a shirt from one of his festivals, threadbare pants probably as old as I am, complete with socks and sneakers. Like all granddaddies he ain't going nowhere, but he is ready to go anyway.

With a big glass of sweet tea sweating on the table next to him, he would be the portrait of any Southern old man if he were not so hideous. I swallow my gasp of shock when I see him. It is no wonder he was mistaken for something other than human.

"Don't be scared girl I don't bite," he croaks out. He has a crooked yellow smile and bloodshot eyes, the corners crinkled with lines, the deep crevices of scaled skin exacerbated by his age, the color mahogany like tree bark.

I take his rough hand in mine, thick discolored nails, and all. "Sorry, Sir. I'm just in awe. You're the first celebrity I've ever met." I hope to smooth over my initial shock with humor. This close he smells like the "OG Spice," the one with the little boat on the bottle. Not the new scents marketed to adolescents with names like "Grizzly Bear Dew Claw" and "Tyrannosaurus Taint."

He chuckles low and deep. "I can't see the best, but I bet you're a pretty little thing."

"Ahhh...neither of those I'm afraid," I reply, causing Marcus to sigh dramatically beside me.

His granddad does not miss a beat. "Not everyone wants roses." He points out toward where the swamp lies through the trees. "All girls are like flowers, pretty in their own way. Out there, there's a Lily that grows right out of that stinking mud. It ain't much. Just long white petals, but it's my favorite, and when I see it...I know I'm home. My Nell, she wasn't a beauty to everyone, but she was to me. So like I was saying, I can't see you too well, but I know you're a beauty, especially to my boy. Now I know it's early but I'm ready to eat."

I cannot argue with that kind of logic. I know all too well about love goggles. I sneak a look at Marcus, and yeah, we both have ours on. He does not give any more shits about the hairs on my chinny-chin-chin than I do about the skin flakes he leaves in my bed.

I send a silent thought and prayer to Miss Innes for teaching me how to make a few things. Of course, she was right I would find someone I want to cook for. Yes, I want to impress Marcus (a little if I am being honest), but the praise I receive from his granddad makes me puff like a peacock. I did not cook anything too fancy, just a *Chicken Bog,* one of the local staples I have added to my list of go-to recipes. Then offered peach cobbler as a dessert, it is one of the 'The Hole's' specialties.

"That was damn good, girl. I haven't had a *Bog* in ages." Marcus' granddad leans back in his chair.

"Well then, would you tell me a story? THE story?" I bat my long eyelashes at him.

"I'm surprised you made it through dinner without asking, honestly," Marcus mumbles to me.

"Ain't much to tell. Tried to help some fool with a flat tire. It was dark and he didn't get too good a look at me. Thought I was some kind of monster that crawled out the swamp. I mean I know I ain't pretty, but a man's got feelings," he laughs.

"I don't know too many people with their very own festival and museum and dance...so there's that," I add gently.

"Damn right there's that," he laughs.

After our nice, but exceedingly early dinner, Marcus and I take the trail at Scape Ore like planned. I picked him up a pair of rubber boots so he would stop ruining his shoes walking here. It is late afternoon, almost evening, but it has been particularly muggy today. Even with October encroaching, we are still having temperatures in the eighties. It is so dry, the swamp has a receding water line exposing more of its muck than I have ever seen. Even the plant life hangs limp and sad.

"Is it just me or does it smell worse than usual?" Marcus voices my own inner thoughts. Usually, it is eau-de-rotten egg...

"It's pretty bad." So bad you can taste it. We do not talk much more than necessary. The smell intensifies the further we go. The bugs scream louder than I remember them ever screaming. Their incessant buzzing is not the only buzz in the air. There seems to be something off.

Dragonflies like always are present; a cluster whizzes by my face. I jerk back so fast I nearly fall into Marcus. He catches my shoulders and rights me. "Easy there."

More dragonflies swarm at the fallen cypress. Here the water line recedes, revealing something protruding from the mire. The drone of insects is chaotic, as is their feeding frenzy. The mass of smaller insects must have been what beckoned the bigger ones.

Just as with the feeling, deep in my gut, that brought me here to this place, I have another. Without getting closer, I just know what that something sticking out of the swamp is.

The Urban Dictionary has a word to define a person who loves true crime. We have been dubbed by pop media and thus the aforementioned slang bible as 'muderinos'. Research has shown that most fanatics of true crime are overwhelmingly women. When asked why, most answer this is because they feel they can learn something from the stories. IE: how to spot a murderer and how to not get murdered themselves.

A self proclaimed "murderino," I have been known to pick up some macabre reading. I once read a study about how different elements affected the buoyancy of human remains in bodies of water. I recently watched a documentary about a body farm that studies decomposition in various elements. And like most people I have seen a dead body, embalmed, and put on display at a funeral. But this...what we are looking at...is so, so wrong, devoid of recognition and defiled.

"Maybe it's a deer." Marcus tries to invent an alternative to what his eyes are seeing.

As the sickening smell hits my olfactory neurons, stomach acid burns its way up my esophagus leaving a fiery trail in its wake. I look down to keep myself from getting sick or worse, passing out. A glint of metal at my feet catches my eye. I reach down to pick up the object, a chandelier earring. This piece of jewelry looks an awful like one I remember seeing on my bar patron while she sipped gin and tonics. I was happy for her that night because she looked like she had a date. Miss Ruby. I curl the fingers of one hand around the earring and the other I wrap around Marcus' arm and pull him away from what is definitely not the rotting carcass of a deer and fear that I picked up (and tampered with) evidence.

XI
Justice

Studies have Found there is a Higher Chance of Missing Persons being Found in Water, Especially if they are Deceased

The last time I sat in this chair is a memory so hazy I do not recall any of the details. I do not remember the ugly oil painting on the wall of a lighthouse. I do not remember these chairs being so mauve or so uncomfortable, well maybe the unease I am feeling comes from the scrutiny I am currently under.

After having explained all of my findings to Travis, shown him the map I made of the missing women, and delivered the earring, I have watched his face turn so many shades of red it is like paint swatches in the home improvement section. Azalea Petal. Ruby Slipper. Cherry Cordial.

He has been pinching the bridge of his nose and taking deep breaths while Marcus and I watch. A vein on his forehead is threatening thrombosis.

He holds up one finger. "So let me get this straight...after watching a true crime documentary you get a hunch, search for missing people from surrounding counties, have a dream that gives you a feeling that takes you to a somewhat remote area BY YOURSELF!" he yells the last part in emphasis. I nod. "Where this guy comes out of fucking nowhere and you don't think that's odd or suspicious at all?"

"I said the same thing," Marcus tries to add.

"You. Don't talk," Travis snaps. He brings his attention back to me. "Continuing with your bullshit...befriend swamp weirdo and continue to go to what feels like an important place." He holds his hands up like he's asking for divine help. "Obviously, you've been hanging around Dontae and his crystals too long," he says sarcastically. "Then you happen to find not only what you believe may be a body, but also an earring you think is Miss Ruby's, which, if that is the case your fingerprints are all over."

"Yeah, I should've known better than to touch that, and yes, that pretty much sums it up," I sniff.

"Do you have any self-preservation? You sound insane!" he yells.

"Cases are solved by amateur sleuths all the time, look at that guy who fucked with cats..." I defend myself.

"I want to throttle you right now," he blurts, all the while rubbing his temples.

"That's not very cop-like," I say.

"As your friend!" he shouts. "What the hell is wrong with you?"

"You guys are friends?" Marcus asks.

"No," I say with conviction.

The same time, Travis says, "Yes, we are." Travis turns his attention to Marcus. "Can you answer something?"

"Of course," Marcus replies.

"Why did you follow a lone woman onto a trail?" His brow raised in suspicion.

Marcus shrugs before answering, "Isn't it obvious? I saw her walking, and I was curious. I wanted to make sure she was okay. Was she meeting someone? Then she turned on me and pulled a knife. I got my first look at the biggest bluest eyes I've ever seen, and I was a goner." He smiles at me, dimple and all.

"You pulled a knife on him?" Travis asks, unsurprisingly.

"It was so hot," Marcus adds.

Travis, done with questioning, starts to make a plan. "First off, the two of you are going to take me to the location. From there, I'll call their county authorities. Neither of you leave the state. You've watched enough shows to know you're both going to be questioned formally, right?"

"Yeah, I figured," I reply.

"And Faye...no more Sherlock shit."

Scape Ore Swamp at night is terrifying. Marcus and I lead Travis and a deputy down the trail with only light beams from our flashlights. The equipment is top notch, but it is still dark and often reflects off the eyes of watching creatures. When we make it to the site, the carcass is still there. It has distended further with bloat and writhes with unseen entities. Travis enters the black water with caution, state issued water resistant boots on his feet. His hands protected with latex gloves; gingerly inspects the waxen mass. When he turns it over, a face appears. Almost unrecognizable as human, the softer bits eaten away. When maggots spill from the empty eye sockets, Marcus turns his head, the deputy projectile vomits, and I am very confused. Even decomposed and partially consumed one thing is for certain, this is no one I have seen before.

Grim Discovery
at Scape Ore Swamp

Lee County—Following an anonymous tip, local authorities discovered human remains in the waters of Scape Ore Swamp late Sunday evening. Law enforcement from several counties have been working together to compile information.

At a press conference this morning it has been stated there have been more than one body found, though authorities are not releasing many details as they are still investigating. The identities of the victims have not been released. The remains are currently in an undisclosed location for DNA testing.

The surrounding area is closed until further notice. Updates will be provided as they are available. Scape Ore Swamp covers approximately 2,200 acres of South Carolina. It is a popular local fishing area. The swamp has gained notoriety nationally with the tale of the Lizardman, a seven-foot tall, red eyed, scaly monster who terrorized the area in 1988.

CHAPTER 21

You are most Likely to be Murdered by Someone you Know

I am so glad this night is almost over. All anyone wants to talk about is our hometown horror story. I am exhausted from dodging as many local gossips as possible.

All my friends have come out to celebrate my last shift. Dontae is at the microphone on stage in a pink velour jumpsuit. "This one is dedicated to you, Faye." As has every karaoke ballad tonight, thanks to the regulars, I feel like maybe I will be missed. I do make a mean Long Island. "When I think about you, I touch myself," Dontae sings, and the entire crowd erupts with laughter.

"Thank you!" I yell over the din.

Haven and the twins sit at the counter. Haven sips a Diet Coke since she agreed to D.D., for the twins I concocted something fruity and easily palatable. I told everyone no fanfare, I am not leaving the state, no dramatics needed. But there was no protest from me when Miss Innes slipped the recipes she had written on index cards into my hands. Written in that beautiful script no longer taught in schools and held together with a rubber band, I will cherish the bundle forever.

Martin is absent. Even after our heart to heart I still find him suspicious. Has he gone into hiding due to current events? Answers are sure to be forthcoming, does he have reason to be nervous? Killers have been notoriously known to make rash choices when they feel pressure, just like rats bite when cornered.

"Hey, Faye," Peyton drawls as I set a cold one in front of him. He grabs my wrist as I move away.

His touch startles me. "Uhhhh... you need something else?"

He releases my arm. "I saw you at the police station. You being naughty?" He smiles and winks.

I sigh. Leave it to Peyton to make any statement sexual. "I was questioned just like every single person around town I assure you."

I turn to help another customer who waved me from further down the bar when he replies, "I heard you found the bodies. What were you doing in that swamp I wonder?"

I do not even give him the satisfaction of a reaction. Dick. This is my last night at "The Hole"—I can do this. Unfortunately, he is unavoidable where he sits so he continues to try and talk to me. "What are you doing after work?"

"Not you." This time, I get as far away as I can, but not before I hear his chuckle.

Cook comes crashing out of the kitchen, the door swings wildly. Even with his face completely tattooed, it is obvious he is distraught. "Faye there's an emergency with one of my Sponsees, I've gotta run to the house and I'll be right back to close with you. Do not walk out of here alone." He high tails it before I can respond.

One thing we never do is let a fellow employee walk out alone. No one is dumb enough to rob the place, if they did, jokes on them; people never pay with cash anymore. There is barely a couple hundred in the safe. We are more likely to have to give an inebriated local yocal a ride or have the misfortune of seeing the bare ass of a patron getting lucky in the parking lot. (No judgement here.) It is in everyone's best interest to not take any unnecessary risks either way.

But as the night winds down, it comes as no surprise that by closing time, Cook has not returned. I have waited long enough. I am officially no longer an employee, and too exhausted to be sad about it. I turn off the lights, set the alarm and leave the last bag of trash since there is no one here to yell at me about it. I am just ready to hit my bed, where Marcus is waiting for me. I am sure I will be fine, as there has never been an incident in all the years, despite it all.

Once my feet touch the parking lot, I pump my legs as fast as they will go towards my car. My purse smacks my side as I hurry. Why did I park so far away? The hair on the back of my neck rises. I chalk it up to normal circumstantial jitters, I am a woman alone in the dark. Though, I get the feeling I am being watched. I swivel my head left and right.

There. In the shadows not touched by the one dim light post, Peyton leans against his truck. I sag with relief. I guess he did not find anyone to go home with or -gag- is looking for seconds.

"Goodnight, Peyton. I'm going home alone," I call out while continuing to speed walk toward my car.

He peels away from his truck and straightens. "You sure?" His accent curiously not as strong as usual.

"Uh yeah, not interested..." Unease lays heavy over my shoulders. "I'm seeing someone." After what felt like an eternity, I finally reach my car.

"That's exactly what Mandy said."

My hand stops on the handle. All the oxygen leaves my lungs. My vision blurs. I sway on my feet. "What?" Confused, I turn to face him.

"Oh come on. You've got a smart mouth; you must have a smart brain to go with it." With these words, his mask slips off completely, and, standing a few feet away, partially obscured in shadows, this person I have known for years becomes a stranger.

I only have a moment to recover from my shock before he closes the distance between us with his long legs and grabs me. I stomp on his foot, but it does nothing. He is wearing steel toed work boots. I kick and thrash until I manage to get my back to him. He continues to drag me towards his four-wheel drive death trap. I flail so erratically it is enough to land an elbow, his grip loosens. I slip out of his arms a second before he has a hold of me again. I scream "fiiiirrrreeeee!" Not "help," because that is what women are taught to do. He slaps a hand over my mouth. I bite down on his flesh. Hard. Have some forensic evidence, bitch! He wrenches away before landing a punch to my face. The hit is so hard I see spots in my vision. He only has one arm around me, I use all my weight to break his hold, then scramble back to my car. Jerking the door open I fall into the seat. My heart is pounding out of my chest. I taste copper as blood fills my mouth and runs down my chin.

The door is just about closed when he rips it wide open. He tries to grab my arm. I claw at his face. He then goes for my legs. I kick wildly. I will not go down without a fucking fight. My keys are in the ignition when he changes tactics and wraps the seatbelt around my neck and pulls it taut.

At this moment I have an out-of-body experience. I hover over the scene watching it all unfold. Peyton leaning into the driver's seat over my body as I struggle. There is no emotion in his chiseled face, his eyes are dead as he calmly watches himself strangle me. Of course it is him. I should have known. Not only would he have an alibi for going to Scape Ore, as he goes there to fish, but his type is always overlooked due to their handsome charm. The old ladies in the church will say, "But he was such a nice boy." (You know who else was a nice boy? Ted Bundy.)

Come to think of it, I always thought his accent was a little over the top. He has been playing sports since he could walk, the head injuries he has suffered would be enough to change anyone's personality.

Faye, are we really psychoanalyzing right now? Don't you dare give up! You haven't even told Marcus you love him. And this would push your dad right over the edge. And your friends would have another missing person to mourn. And there is that new movie coming out next month with that hot guy fighting zombies...

Pain snaps me back into my body. I reach around my car feeling for anything that can be used as a weapon. My fingers brush the console, I blindly search inside finding nothing but condiment packets. Wait, there is something cold, cylinder shaped. My lungs ache with the need to breathe. I flick the cap off the container, squeeze my eyes shut and blast my attacker in the face with the bear spray I bought after Marcus warned me.

I haul ragged breaths into my burning lungs. Peyton is rubbing his face with his shirt. I am not surprised he is not particularly phased, my Nanny always said, "Crazy people are stronger than normal people." She was like a hundred and always said kooky shit like that, but here is a lunatic about to come at me again as I struggle to make up for lost oxygen. I slam my door, start my engine, and begin to drive off. But...

I see that motherfucker in my rear-view mirror, and something happens. A red haze washes over me. I am not scared anymore. I am fucking mad. I shift into reverse and floor it. For Mandy. For anyone scared to walk alone in the dark. For me.

He tries to move out of my way, but I still barrel into his ass. He bounces off my bumper, the crunching sound loud and satisfying. I shift into drive and stomp on the gas. The adrenaline that has fueled me through this ordeal is fizzling out, the lack of oxygen and punch to the face catches up with me, and I lose control of my vehicle. It slams into Peyton's truck. I do not get to see if he rises like a knife-toting psycho. I slump over my horn as it blares into the night, and everything fades to black.

CHAPTER 22

I Survived

"Wake up Sleepyhead," Marcus whispers in between the soft kisses he feathers across my cheeks. I open my eyes to meet his green ones. They practically twinkle with mirth. His hair is shorter and slicked back with pomade. I like the fresh look. So much I drag his mouth to mine and deepen my affection.

We get lost in each other for a moment before he pulls away, "Save that for later or you'll be late," his breathing unsteady.

"Late for what?" I ask. He takes my hand and pulls me to my feet. I take in my surroundings. His trousers are held up with black suspenders over a crisp white shirt. Continuously smiling, his dimple on full display. He leads me through the red and white flaps of my tent to a dazzling sight outside.

"Your party," Marcus answers, while gesturing toward a table. It has been set up in the middle of the surrounding tents. Yellow string lights zig and zag between them shining their soft glow on everyone I love.

The Little Shits, the Dwarves, beam at me. Next to them, Haven, the Lobster Girl, her ringlets gilded even more so in the party lights. Quinn and Tillie, here joined at the hip like Siamese Twins, move in the choreographed dance only they know. Travis, his muscles oiled and on full display in a leopard print cloth, the Strongman. Cook, the Tattooed Man. Trevor, the Thin boy. Miss Irene, the Fat Lady. And Miss Innes in a top hat, the Magician. My dad, in a red and black jacket, the Ring Master. My oldest niece dressed in a monkey suit perched on his lap. Dontae walks out from between two tents holding an enormous pink and white cake. "It's not my birthday." R.B. jumps on the table, a ruffled collar around his neck.

"After what you went through, we thought you deserved a party," Dontae replies while setting the cake on the table. His long flowing skirt swooshes as he comes to my side. "Everyone is here."

Marcus squeezes my hand, his eyes full of love, my Lizardman. "Not everyone is here, where's Mandy?" I ask.

Dontae pulls a tarot card from the folds of his skirt and holds it out for me. Dontae, the Fortune Teller.

"It's Death." I hold the card out, skeleton facing out for all to see. "But you said Death doesn't mean an actual death."

Dontae looks at me sadly, "This time it does."

"Am I dead too?" Tears trail down my cheeks catching in my thick beard. Me, the Bearded Lady.

"No, just another one of your lucid dreams," he smiles at me. "And I think it's time to wake up."

"But everyone is here," I whine.

Marcus brings our linked hands to his mouth and brushes his lips over my knuckles. "No, Faye, everyone's waiting."

Slowly, I rise to the surface to the sounds of beeping monitors, playing their hospital melody. My entire body aches, especially my throat and face.

"Hey." I turn my head towards the voice. Travis perches on the edge of the chair beside my bed.

I try to speak, only a croak comes out of me. Travis puts a water bottle in my hand. The room temperature liquid feels like the blade of a knife when I swallow. My split lip is tight, trying to mend.

"It's every girl's fantasy to have a disheveled man vigilant at their bedside, but no offense, I was hoping for a different man," my voice raspy. "I sound sexy."

Travis laughs. "I sent Marcus home to eat and shower. He's been driving me nuts."

"How long have I been here?" All the memories from the attack come rushing into my mind. I feel the aches and pains throughout my body.

"Two days. Faye, what the hell happened?" He runs his hands over his face, exhaustion etched in every line.

"Where's Peyton?" I answer his question with the most important question of all.

"In a hospital one county over attempting to press aggravated assault charges on you," he answers. "He claims you came after him with some wild accusations and then hit him with your car."

I try to protest but he holds his hand up.

"But his skin is under your nails, you took a nasty punch to the face and the bruises around your neck show you were strangled. So Faye, I ask again, what the hell happened?"

"Travis...I think he killed Mandy," I whisper.

"Please don't tell me you went after him on another one of your crazy hunches." He looks up to the ceiling to gain composure.

"No. He said something weird just before he attacked me." I take another drink to soothe my throat. "I was just as surprised as you are right now."

"I've known him my whole life." Travis looks at me, completely lost. "But I also know what defensive wounds look like. That's why I didn't believe his side of the story."

"What happens now?" I ask weakly.

"You'll need to come to the station and give me every single detail of the night's events. I've got to make a case for a warrant. We'll keep an eye on him...and you." He rubs his eyes.

"You should get some rest first," I rasp.

"I don't think I'd be able to sleep, even if I tried," he answers. We sit quietly a moment before he says, "We're hiring at the station. Now that you are no longer bartending, and you like crime and punishment so much."

"Jesus Christ, no. Why would you say that? I don't like donuts that much." I am horrified at his suggestion. "The only crime I want in my life is from the safety of my couch."

"Why? Don't you think it's depressing." He is judging me. I can see it.

"Murder shows remind me I am still alive. And I owe it to those who aren't to not take that for granted." *And now... especially now that I could have been one of the victims.*

A nurse comes in exclaiming with excitement when she sees me awake and checks my vitals.

"You know *you* are one lucky girl," she says.

Shuffling at the entry to my room draws my attention. Marcus stands there with his whole heart in his eyes. They shine with unshed tears. He loves me so much.

"Yeah don't I know it."

Chapter 23
What Astrological Sign is your Soulmate? Click Here to take the Test and Find Out

I spent another twenty-four hours in the hospital after waking. I did not have any considerable damage, thankfully. Just shook up, inside and out.

Since returning to my apartment, I have continued my convalescence in my own bed for another two days. I have not left the comfort of my black and gray bedspread, and I have what can only be called a ten o'clock shadow. Marcus runs the tips of his fingers along my scruffy jaw, "You're still the most beautiful girl to me." He must be reading my thoughts. He has not left my side since my release from the hospital, choosing to wait on me hand and foot.

"Put your glasses on," I mumble my reply.

"Don't talk about my best fiend like that," he says from my chest where he uses my bosom as a pillow. "It really doesn't bother me. You know that, right?"

"Yeah I do. You know I love you, right?" I look down at him.

"Well, yeah. What's not to love?" He buries his face further into my cleavage and starts nibbling.

As he presses his hips into mine, I groan, "You are not possibly ready to go again."

"I'm young and spry, remember?" He gives me the side smile he knows I have a hard time refusing.

"At what age do I trade you in?"

His answer is a playful swat to side. "Today is going to be weird."

I ruin the mood by bringing attention to the fact he is meeting my bedridden father today. My family was only given vague and brief details of what happened to me, as to not upset him. Or them, truly, they have enough on their plate to deal with.

"It's okay. I want to do this." He moves higher up so we are eye to eye. He tenderly caresses the purple and green bruises on my neck. He follows the touch of his fingers with his lips, and we stay like that until it is time to leave.

"What exactly are your intentions with Sissy?" Kyle asks of Marcus. He is so puffed up it is comical.

"Dude he's already defiled me, no need to duel at dawn," I laugh as Kyle winces at my crude reply. Marcus looks bashful making me cackle harder. We are on the back porch of my childhood home. I have just introduced Marcus to Kyle and Scarlet and given them a cliff notes version of the other night's happenings. I also need a moment to prepare myself for going inside and seeing my parents. I know my mother will look at Marcus, judging his appearance, just like she does mine. I need to strengthen my resolve so I do not go on the defensive and say something ignorant. Not that she doesn't deserve it, but my dad does not.

Inside, it is quiet. My mother is fussing in the kitchen like always, not a hair out of place. The perfect God-fearing Southern wife. My dad sits, propped up with a plethora of pillows, nearly skeletal. His dull eyes light up when he sees us walk in, until he notices the bruises and scabbed lip. "Pumpkin." He says my nickname with so much sadness. I fall into his open arms. "How could anyone hurt my Pumpkin? I'm so glad you're okay," he says into my hair. His hold on me physically weak, though no less comforting.

"Can I get you anything?" My mother plays hostess behind me. I hear Marcus say, "No, thank you," and introduce himself. Whatever she thinks of him, there is no denying my boyfriend has impeccable manners.

After a minute, my dad releases me. "Alright let's meet your gentleman," he says as strongly as he can. Marcus moves over to his bedside and shakes his hand. "Wish we could have met in better circumstances," my dad says. Tears streak my freshly shaven face. I wouldn't dare walk in here without shaving. My mother would have a field day. I would not give her the satisfaction. My peace is important to me.

I try to eaves drop on their low conversation, but am unsuccessful. I see Marcus nodding along to whatever my dad says. I feel my mother watching me, I look over to where she stands.

She says, "I know you won't believe me, but I am glad you're okay."

We do not embrace; it is not our way. I simply nod. And I realize...I am okay. Things do not always play out the way we hope or expect, but we humans are so much stronger than we think. I am stronger than I thought. I am a little worse for wear, but I did not break completely. Marcus looks at me and smiles, maybe I am a little better than just okay.

Epilogue

"You won't fucking believe it...the girls did our story on their podcast," I tell the pink glass bead I am fingering at my neck with one hand and the vial of gray dust I hold in the other. "I told them to say you didn't light up a room and a lot of people thought you were a bitch," I cackle loudly and dig my toes into the sand. I am not a beach girl.

Marcus and I are in folding chairs under an umbrella, hiding from UV rays. Martin is in a chair not far from us, getting two shades darker.

"He's not that bad," Marcus chuckles next to me. "I get what you saw in him. He's pretty hot."

"So, they found you in the swamp. And Miss Ruby, too... what was left. I have some of you here so you could finally get to Florida." I start to cry.

Marcus puts his hand on my knee and gives it a comforting squeeze.

Mandy's parents gave me a packet of her ashes to spread here. Not in the water though, the time she spent in water was long enough. I am spreading her here on the warm sandy beach to be kissed by sun rays for all of time.

I saved a pinch of her ashes for me; it has been turned into the cremation bead I wear on a silver chain. Mandy wanted to travel, so I will take her with me everywhere I go. Next month we're going to Tennessee. I am finally going to see some mountains.

The bead is pink, her favorite color. The exact shade of the acrylic nail found between the seat cushions in Peyton's truck. The nail that was somehow missed in his extensive cleaning and had Mandy's DNA on it. Once the investigators found his 'trophies,' he was officially charged.

"You'd like Marcus. I wish you guys could've met. You'd say he was too nice though..." My tears fall in earnest. "He asked me to marry him, but I said no. My Maid of Honor isn't here. I think I'd miss my last name, I want to keep it in memory of my dad. In typical Marcus fashion though, he said he'd take my last name instead. I still said no, and in typical Faye fashion I got his name tattooed on my ass."

"I got yours too," Marcus adds.

"I miss you so much. You didn't deserve what happened to you. You should be here with us. I hope they have good salons wherever you are. And good coffee," I sniff.

The sky is a cloudless blue. The sun rays twinkle over the gulf. A light breeze tickles my bare legs. It is what I imagine Mandy's heaven would look like.

A dragonfly meanders over to perch on the metal arm of my beach chair. I glance at my other tattoo, a dragonfly on my wrist, a 'M' curlicued in the wing. Martin nods to me. I uncap the bottle and sprinkle the ash into the air. I know it is probably my imagination, but it looks like glitter as the particles intermingle with grain after grain of sand.

Thanks.
Gracias. Danke. Merci. Arigato.
AND THIRTY MORE WAYS TO SAY THANK YOU.

I think I need to start this out with, "I can't believe I wrote another book!" Or maybe, "I can't believe I wrote *this* book." This one you're holding. It has been the easiest book to write, but the hardest book to share. This book has so much ME in it. Working retail and in food service, watching someone I love in hospice, and having sarcasm as my native language... but also I know it's a little weird. But if you've read anything else I've written, you know my head is a strange place and I hope you don't mind it in there.

True crime got me through the first hard year of perimenopause. Looking in a mirror and not recognizing yourself, angry and depressed for no reason other than estrogen and sweating...so much sweating. So it is a big theme in this book, as well as the trials and tribulations of menstruation. It seems odd to me that this cycle is still a little taboo, when so many people you are around are literally experiencing it every single day. (And yes I said people— all genders menstruate.) Same as this new mid-life journey I am on. Let me say this, it is ok to talk about it. It is ok to ask for help. It is ok to realize you may not be ok. You are not alone.

Indie Authors have it hard, but we get by with a lot of help from our friends. Suzanne Shelden, thank you for publishing my books. Without you I would never have this very special piece of myself. I'm not sure I will be able to say thank you enough. But I'll try.

To Overthinkers Anonymous...you guys. What a rag tag bunch of weirdos?! What an incredibly talented group of friends. Everyone needs a writing group. I will die on this hill. Thank you

Heather for opening your bookstore doors to give us a home and all of the support you give to our writing and all you do for me.

Frances. You need to start charging me for reading everything I send your way. You're one of my favorite people ever, especially because we had to have a safe word for when you speak in public.

Jess. You don't read a lot, but you always read my books. Literally can't ask for more in a ride or die. Looking forward to growing old with you since you are stuck with me for life.

Cierra I have to be honest I had you beta read my book because you weren't the biggest fan of my last one. I was hoping you'd give me insight as to why and help get this one off to a good start. Thank you for reading deeply and sending notes my way and all of your support. I hope you find your dangly earring wearing hockey player one day.

Lucy thank you also for beta reading. I am ready to return the favor so get to writing. I can't wait to see you hold your own book.

To those who got an arc of this book but didn't have the chance to finish no worries.... Life gets busy and I am a high maintenance friend.

Thank you to you guys, my readers, for the continuing support. It is wild and scary to share my stories, but I just can't help myself. I love words. I love to write. But to be honest, I may have given up without your encouragement. So thank you.

And I wouldn't be able to follow this dream, run a business and have a house full of teenagers without the the best partner a gal could ask for. Joe, you really are the best husband. You guys have no idea how much murder podcast recap he has had to listen to.

To my kids I promise I'll dedicate my next book to you.

About the Author

Jen Poteet is a creative thinker and doer dwelling on the edge of the Blue Ridge Mountains with her husband, Joe, their kids, and a menagerie of pets. When she isn't daydreaming or exploring, she can be found at Black Sheep Studios, the tattoo studio and art gallery she owns and operates with Joe. Her other books include: *Bones Picked Clean,* a story taking place deep in the Appalachian Mountains; *Secondhand Heart,* a quirky romcom for fellow weirdos; and *A Night Under the Circus Tent,* an illustrated children's book.